A Golden Opportunity

J MARIE CROFT

This is a work of fiction. Names, characters, businesses, places, events, locales, and incidents are either the products of the author's imagination or used in a fictitious manner. Any resemblance to actual persons, living or dead, or actual events is purely coincidental.

Edited by Debbie Styne and Mary McLaughlin

Book cover designed by Trisha Fuentes

ISBN 978-1-963213-01-0 (ebook) 978-1-963213-02-7 (paperback)

To paraphrase Sir P. G. Wodehouse:
This novella is dedicated to my husband Dennis, without whose never-failing encouragement, assistance, and interruptions this book would have been finished in half the time.

Prologue

March 7, 1812

Miss Anne de Bourgh resided in what could only be called the world's most tiresome place, a place of such abundant leisure that almost any sort of novelty was a welcome change.

As though that were not misfortune enough, the spring weather did not know how to be anything other than unseasonably frigid. She had been kept within doors, unable to enjoy the freedom of driving her phaeton and consulting the master gardener about specimens for her herbarium, a pastime that was naught but an excuse to visit Gilchrist's cottage and beyond.

Her cousins had yet to arrive, though she suspected they would make little difference when they did present themselves on the twenty-third. Albeit the colonel could be entertaining at times, Darcy and Anne had blessed little in common, save for the fact both were dreadful company on a Sunday evening when there was nothing to do.

At the heart of the matter, there was a world out there which Anne very much longed to explore and experience.

While awaiting those who had been invited to dine, she was overcome with listlessness and dissatisfaction arising from lack of occupation. Sitting and silently snivelling, she stifled another yawn and listened while her mother and Mrs Jenkinson, whom Anne considered two of the world's most exasperating old women, discussed the upcoming ball. Although the celebration would be held in her honour, Anne was permitted little in the way of involvement and, therefore, was ill-disposed to be pleased by anything they suggested.

Unseen and unheard beneath her skirts, the toes of her slippers tapped in time as the hands of the nearby clock ticked towards six. Such impatience was pointless. Anne expected little novelty upon the Hunsford party's arrival though she, at least, might have been unintentionally entertained by the tedious rector. Either that or at the dinner table, she would fall fast asleep headfirst, blowing bubbles in her turtle soup.

Being a genteel young lady, she hesitated to describe Mr Collins as a lickspittle, but he was excessively attentive to anything remotely concerning Lady Catherine de Bourgh.

From the entrance hall the parson's voice, as oily as his pomade, drifted Anne's way. A glance at the mantel confirmed the punctilious cleric was nothing if not punctual. He swept into the room and into a ridiculously low obeisance before his patroness.

Perhaps the graceless fellow will fall flat on his face this time.

Concealing unseemly mirth behind an ever-present handkerchief, Anne prayed the crinkling corners of her eyes and the shaking of her shoulders remained unnoticed. After all, she was supposed to be sullen and in poor health.

How could anyone presently residing on this estate be anything other than miserable? That thought brought Mr Collins's hapless wife to mind. *What a prodigious wealth of patience she must possess.*

Once Mrs Collins had introduced her houseguests, her father, Sir William Lucas, seemingly awed by the grandeur surrounding him, made a courtly bow as though he were at St James's. Then he took a seat without saying a word. The man's younger daughter, Miss Maria Lucas, appeared frightened almost out of her senses while being made known to Lady Catherine.

The poor girl is even more of a mouse than I am purported to be.

But Miss Elizabeth Bennet, Mrs Collins's friend and distant cousin of her husband, appeared quite equal to the task of bearing up admirably in front of Lady Catherine, all the while remaining polite without resorting to affectation. Anne thought the girl had more pluck than the harp that stood unused in the corner.

Such a pert and pretty young woman brings a much-needed

freshness and lightness to this stale, dim room. I find her a fascinating creature.

Miss Bennet did not behave according to the most current fashion nor did she dress in that manner, though Anne hardly would have known what was or was not in vogue were it not for her own lady's maid, Dubois. Still, Miss Bennet possessed a particular sort of elegance and charm. Such style was in direct opposition to the dowdiness and vapidity enforced on Anne by her overbearing mother, and she was less and less inclined to endure the restraints imposed by her ladyship.

Next month, however, all such parental strictures may be cast aside.

Anne viewed the formal drawing room through the young lady's dark eyes. While Miss Bennet studied the frescoed ceiling, Anne followed suit and noticed, perhaps for the first time in her life, that the elaborate scene was engirdled by an aureate cornice. Its golden curves, spirals, and flourishes fascinated her, and straightaway she conceived an inspiring notion. In her mind's eye, she pictured the end result, and it was glorious.

Coincidentally, thanks to Dubois—a French émigré of the Revolution of 1789 and a Kentish cousin of the late Sir Lewis de Bourgh—a few of the materials Anne would require for her creation already were in her possession. That little diversion of theirs recently had saved her from a monotonous routine and a humdrum, cheerless existence. They considered their handiwork a lark. Others called it vandalism or out-and-out thievery.

What nonsense! I own Rosings Park. Ergo, I cannot steal from myself.

Days prior, when their mischief had first been detected, the person most affected by it ranted and raved and cried, "Heaven and earth! This is an outrage! I shall know how to act!"

In consequence, the magistrate was summoned. Servants were questioned and their quarters searched by the butler and housekeeper under her ladyship's supervision. Nothing was brought to light. Anne, Dubois, and Mrs Jenkinson may have been delinquent, but they were resourceful and clever.

Despite that recent upset, an extravagant celebration was to proceed as planned. Preparations had been underway for weeks. Lavish invitations had been dispatched to those Lady Catherine most wished to impress and to those by whose presence Anne would be honoured.

You are cordially invited to a private ball in celebration of Miss Anne de Bourgh's twenty-first birthday to take place at Rosings Park, Kent, on Monday evening, April 20, commencing at nine o'clock.

Chapter One

Friday, April 10, 1812

Outside Rosings Park's stable at daybreak, Fitzwilliam Darcy stood holding Cadogan's reins, knowing he had but a moment to decide whether it was nobler to suffer in silence or to confess a staggering failure.

Could his favourite cousin's pity or the slings and arrows of his teasing be endured? No, Darcy was of a disposition to tolerate neither commiseration nor ridicule.

Nobly suffering in silence it will be then. No one else must ever know of my vain attempt. Except her, of course. Still, he thought it would have been gratifying to have had the colonel's assurance that he in no way resembled the uncomplimentary portrait of him painted the previous evening.

"So, after only three weeks, you are deserting us,

leaving me to deal with"—Darcy's head twitched towards the manor—"them."

"Sorry, old chap." Colonel Fitzwilliam was in the process of adjusting his horse's girth, so it was debatable whether his apology was meant for Cadogan or Darcy. "Speaking of deserting, where the devil did you go last evening? I thought you might have been at the parsonage entertaining a certain pert young lady who dared decline our aunt's invitation to drink tea."

Yes, I went there, only to be scathingly spurned by that pert young lady—the woman I ardently admire and love. Darcy's indignant huff formed a cloud in the frosty air. *Admired and loved. Past tense.*

He knew he was fooling no one, least of all himself. He loved her still, in spite of the heartache she had caused, but her rejection was akin to bereavement, a loss as keenly felt as the untimely deaths of his parents. From those experiences, he knew grief would become less painful over time. That morning though it hurt deeply, to his very soul. Furthermore, his pride had taken an awful beating at her hands.

In response to his cousin's enquiry, Darcy scoffed. "Engaging Miss Elizabeth Bennet? I should think not." Forcing his eyes from the direction of the parsonage where she remained a guest, he rubbed Cadogan's neck with strong, rhythmic strokes. "If you must know, I went for a ride." *A wild, reckless gallop that did naught to soothe this hellish anguish.*

Although a groom already had done so, the colonel

bent to inspect his horse's hooves. "I hope you enjoyed your freedom, Darcy, because let me tell you, once the Hunsford party left, there was neither pleasure nor escape to be had. Lady Catherine subjected me to her wrath. How was I even remotely responsible for your dereliction of duty?"

Surmising the colonel was accountable for information of which Darcy would have preferred Elizabeth remained unaware, he felt not a whit of sympathy for him.

Serves you right, you meddling rat.

"She even criticised my superiors for summoning me away from Anne's forthcoming celebration. I only managed to beat a hasty retreat when she ceased haranguing me long enough to take an overdue breath."

Tilting his head skywards, Darcy released another huff and watched the exhalation dissipate into nothingness, just as his hopes had done. *You had it easy, my friend. Last evening I endured bitter criticism from not one but two women. To be rejected! And with so little endeavour at civility.*

After his punishing ride, as soon as the manor's front door had closed behind him, Darcy had been accosted by Lady Catherine.

"Nephew! I insist you put aside your bachelor ways, do your duty, and marry my daughter."

Et cetera, et cetera, et cetera. Her breath had been entirely wasted on him. Confronted with that same old claptrap, he had responded in a disrespectful tone and was summarily dismissed. Retreating to his bedchamber, he had poured himself a large rummer of brandy—then another. Not a drop of solace was found in the bottom of the glass, only a swimming head and waves of umbrage and broken-heartedness.

Recollecting himself, Darcy handed the reins to his cousin. "Since events at Ramsgate, I have hardly known the blessing of a single tranquil hour." But upon encountering Elizabeth in Kent, he had hoped his life was about to take a turn for the better. Why could he not have that which he most desired?

"Well, Cousin, as Claudius said in *Hamlet*, 'When sorrows come, they come not single spies but in battalions'." The colonel heaved himself upon the saddle. "You know I would stay longer and help you investigate the bizarre goings-on hereabouts, if at all possible, but unfortunately for both of us, duty calls. Just remember, if things are going untowardly one month, they are sure to mend the next." He tipped his hat and trotted off towards London and his own regiment of battalions.

Longing to be away himself, Darcy kept watch until his cousin disappeared from view.

When sorrows and troubles come, they come not single spies but as the women in my life—Georgiana, Lady Catherine, Anne, and last but certainly not least, the irrepressible Miss Elizabeth Bennet. Interwoven with his tangle with the latter young lady, the knots created by his female relations needed unravelling.

Squaring his shoulders, he made for the house. Veering from the front door, he sneaked in through the garden entrance, thus avoiding another confrontation with his aunt, though he doubted she would be awake until much later.

The manor quietly hummed with activity as maids and footmen went about their duties—opening shutters, cleaning ashes and soot from grates, sweeping, dusting, polishing, and myriad other tasks. But they might as well have been invisible as Darcy passed by them, lost in thought.

Clearly, he had been out of his senses to pay addresses to a young lady of lower standing. Moreover, Elizabeth Bennet was out of her senses to have refused him. As conceit and indignation rose within his breast, Darcy considered how fortunate he was to have escaped such inequality. And he told himself, while hastening up the staircase, that particular thought had nothing at all to do with Aesop's sour grapes.

A lesser man might have felt his life as tragic as *Hamlet,* the play from which Colonel Fitzwilliam had quoted.

At least, unlike Shakespeare's tale, there are no dead bodies littering the place. Yet.

Darcy had a letter to write, and he would attempt to be civil about it, even if it killed him.

It was done. Three hours had passed since he had awakened at five to bid his cousin farewell and to compose a response to Elizabeth's allegations. Not of an inclination to mince words, Darcy's bitterness had spewed forth upon two sheets of hot-pressed letter paper and spilled over onto the envelope page.

The ink was sanded and the sheaf folded with precision. Quality sealing wax, scented with cloves and balsam, was melted above the candle, releasing an aroma evocative of Christmas. Despite his expectations to the contrary, Pemberley would *not* have a delightful mistress presiding over Yuletide festivities that year.

Once the wax was applied to the paper, the taper's flame was snuffed between wetted thumb and forefinger. His eyes watered, and he denied the sting had anything to do with other than the smoking candle.

If ever I marry, it will be for affection and connexions, not for some grand love. With undue force, the Darcy intaglio was stamped into the warm, red blob, thus sealing both the letter and his fate. *Love—a daft, fanciful notion!*

Stepping away from the desk, he flexed cramped fingers and donned his superfine coats. A glance at the pier glass revealed a pale, drawn face with shadows beneath the eyes. Tucked into a breast pocket, the letter weighed him down like the celestial sphere resting upon Atlas's shoulders. Even under that encumbrance, Darcy walked tall and with confidence as he left the bedchamber.

How he wished he could escape as his cousin had done —flee, sneak away from the monstrosity of a house. Just go, and let them sort out their own problems. At times, family duty was a damnable millstone round one's neck.

Descending the stairs, he wondered how a person could be filled with emptiness.

Now I am adrift, off course. Thrown over. Cast aside like so much rubbish into the sea. But there was a lifeline, a rope tethering him. Duty to Georgiana and to Pemberley would save him from being carried along in a strong current, as some of his dissolute peers were apt to do.

With several collars hindering all attempts to rub away tenseness in his nape and with the hatband pressing into his aching skull, Darcy left the house and advanced towards Elizabeth's favourite walk.

Upon arrival, he stood reminiscing. *We used to meet here and—*

Unbidden, an image of her angry face superimposed itself behind his squeezed-shut eyes. At variance with his feelings, she never had cherished their frequent encounters and rambles together. How could he have been so terribly wrong about her opinion of him? At least he had learnt that she, of all the Bennets, was not mercenary.

An endlessly dull, barren world loomed on the horizon. A bleak future seemed imminent. Nevertheless, as he strode eastwards into the rising sun, Darcy had to admit the weeks spent in Kent had made a noticeable difference in the budding of the early trees. The countryside was not as lifeless as it seemed.

Having already postponed his departure several times, he had planned to leave the following day but was compelled to remain at Rosings—not in accordance with Lady Catherine's edict but for his cousin Anne's sake.

Never would he have agreed to stay for the ball had he known his proposal would be rejected, but not once had such a possibility entered Darcy's mind. If he remembered correctly, Elizabeth was to depart on the eighteenth.

Perhaps her own departure will be brought forward, sparing me the agony of the woman's prolonged presence. He had gone from wanting her forever by his side to wanting her gone from his sight.

After pacing for half an hour along her preferred route and eventually assuming she, contriving to avoid him, had steered clear of that particular walk, he abandoned any hope of encountering Elizabeth that morning.

How foolish I was to expend time and energy writing to a young lady so wholly unconnected with me.

Cringing at the dreadful bitterness of spirit in which the letter had been written, Darcy intended to consign the missive to a good blaze upon return to his room. His words would be burnt to a crisp, leaving nothing but charred remains, like the remnants of his ill-fated aspirations.

Not yet wanting to return to the manor and the people therein, he ambled along the lane towards blooming wild cherry trees. Even their white, frothy flowers failed to gladden his heart.

When visiting his de Bourgh relations as a youth and wanting to escape Lady Catherine's tirades, he often had run to the wooded paths far beyond the park, so he directed his steps thus.

Perhaps I wandered here this morning to escape the memory of another woman's verbal onslaught. The voice he previously had thought so endearingly sweet had turned harsh twelve hours earlier. Raised in vitriol, it had accused him of numerous shortcomings. In a tone as sharp as a honed dagger, her final insult had been that he was the last man in the world whom she ever could be prevailed on to marry. *The last man! Was she mad?*

Upon entering the woods, a shaft of sunlight shone through the trees, stabbing his bleary eyes. Tipping his brim downwards and in such affliction as rendered him careless to his surroundings, Darcy watched his boots make long strides. A robin's song could not compete against Elizabeth Bennet's voice repeatedly ringing in his ears. *'Your arrogance...conceit...selfish disdain of the feelings of others...so immoveable a dislike...I had not known you a month before I felt that you were—'*

"Mr Darcy!"

Egad. The self-same young lady who had occasioned the extinction of all his dearest hopes was standing alongside the path.

Bathed in dappled light, she was heartbreakingly lovely. What a pretty picture she made standing there! He thought even the most gifted portraitist could not do justice to her loveliness, and his heart broke anew. *Yesterday I was certain to be engaged to her, ecstatically so, by now.*

Someday, some fortunate man would win her hand, and Darcy could not help but despise him for it. In his chest, the organ that had grown tender ached from loss and wounded pride, but vestiges of anger remained.

I shall be the epitome of gentlemanliness and charm, and she soon will regret her refusal.

Darcy knew he was deluding himself, for he was wracked more by sadness and mortification than vindictiveness. Still, he wished her a lifetime of happiness. Could she perceive from his countenance all she had wrought?

They looked upon one another, and he fell into the fathomless depths of warm, brown eyes until she moved past him.

"Madam, wait!" His tone, even to his own ears, sounded snappish.

Chapter Two

Oppressed by a host of differing emotions, not the least of which were anger and indignation, Elizabeth slowly turned back towards the gentleman and responded with exaggerated impertinence.

"We are to continue last evening's mode of incivility, are we? Very well. I beg your pardon, but no, in the interests of graciousness, I think it best I not linger. Good day to you, sir." She dropped a negligible curtsey and walked away.

Mr Darcy's voice followed. "Please, Miss Bennet. I require but a moment of your time."

Elizabeth never thought herself wanting in self-possession, but even with a tolerably stout heart and a good dose of fortitude, she had had quite enough of Mr Darcy to last a lifetime. In her own defence, his insulting proposal had come on the heels of Colonel Fitzwilliam's information that his cousin had congratulated himself on having saved a friend, Mr Bingley, from the inconveniences of a most imprudent marriage—meaning to her sister Jane. *Congratulated himself! Such arrogance!*

For five weeks, her sojourn in Kent had passed pleasantly, if uneventfully. Then everything changed when the prideful Mr Darcy—whom she assumed had been pledged to Miss de Bourgh—had asked her, with nary a complimentary word, to be his wife.

Guilt, sharp and unwelcome, now halted her escape. In good conscience, Elizabeth knew she had behaved no better than a termagant the previous evening, and no matter how much he might deserve it, she would not subject him to the same unduly harsh treatment again.

As she turned to face Mr Darcy, she chastised herself for so cruelly rejecting him. Not for a minute did she rue her refusal of his offer, but she owed him an apology.

I may as well give the man his moment, express my regrets, then take my leave of him. After what passed between them, the less time spent in one another's company the better.

To his credit, Mr Darcy seemed disinclined to disturb the wretchedness of her mind with idle conversation. Such never was his wont.

"I have been wandering about in the hope of meeting you." Reaching into a breast pocket, he spoke with aplomb. "Will you do me the honour of reading this?"

Determined to display no further symptoms of pique, Elizabeth instinctively accepted the letter, though she looked at it as though it might bite her. "Whose messenger are you this morning, sir? Historically, such envoys have come to grievous harm when bearing bad tidings."

"Ah yes, shooting the messenger, a time-honoured response to news as unwanted as my amorous addresses." Averting his eyes, Mr Darcy scrubbed a gloved palm across his mouth. "I beg your pardon. That was uncalled for. As for shooting the messenger, I remain unafraid of you." A fleeting smile failed to reach his eyes. "And whether the contents of that letter are to your liking or not, they are meant merely to serve as explanations of past events. Without expectation, it is my hope that after a perusal, you might alter your perception of me and my behaviour."

"This is from *you*?" She scowled at the epistle before pushing it towards Mr Darcy's chest. "I cannot possibly accept it." When he—childishly, in her opinion—hid both hands behind his back, Elizabeth had no choice but to keep possession of the letter. Dropping it to the forest floor and grinding it beneath her heel would be preposterous.

The gentleman's next words were spoken with what seemed to her a degree of urgency. "There is vital information therein pertaining to Mr Wickham. Before you return to Hertfordshire, you must be informed of that man's dangerous propensities. You, your sisters, your friends, Meryton merchants—everyone—should be made aware of Wickham's habits and history. I regret not doing so while at Netherfield, but I had other people and their reputations to protect."

Doubtful, Elizabeth gave him a searching look before

nodding and placing the letter inside her pelisse's pocket. Seemingly satisfied, he offered a perfunctory obeisance and was about to turn away from the plantation when her words halted him.

"Colonel Fitzwilliam noticed Charlotte and me gathering eggs earlier this morning and stopped to bid us farewell. I was sorry to see him go."

Mr Darcy's tone was unmistakably surly when he replied. "Yes, I am sure you feel ill-used by so forced a relinquishment."

Although temptation was strong, she refrained from kicking the gentleman's shin. *I am making an effort to bury the tumult of my feelings beneath the restraint of society. Can he not do the same?* "The colonel informed me that you are unable to depart tomorrow as planned." *God willing, you and I, however, shall part now and for evermore.* "I assume you are to remain for Miss de Bourgh's ball."

Their fraught history notwithstanding, Elizabeth thought they should be perfectly capable of conversing like well-bred gentlefolk. *Let us see how long it may last.*

In keeping with his customary mien, Mr Darcy replied in a dispassionate tone. "I am, yes. On the twentieth we shall celebrate my cousin's birthday. Apart from that, there are certain matters at Rosings requiring my attention. And you? Will you stay and attend the celebration?"

In defiance of the awkwardness in which she found herself, Elizabeth forced amiability into her voice. "Lady Catherine graciously invited me to the event and was rather put out that I would not delay my departure.

However, my travel arrangements were made well in advance, and I shall leave as scheduled on the eighteenth. It is with regret that I shall not be here for Miss de Bourgh's special day, but I am eager to be with Jane in London." A calm demeanour could not draw a veil over the angry accusation brimming within her eyes. "As you fully are aware, late in November my beloved sister suffered a devastating disappointment. Since then, she has contended with misery of the acutest kind."

Elizabeth thought it entirely possible she, herself, was more indignant over Mr Bingley's desertion than even her elder sister. *Jane weeps. I fume. What was it his royal highness said at Hunsford? 'I have no wish of denying I did everything in my power to separate my friend from your sister or that I rejoice in my success.' Hateful man!* "Mr Darcy, I regret—"

From behind, heavy, hurried footfalls sounded on the path. As she turned, one of Rosings Park's liveried footmen came to a panting, bowing halt before her.

"Miss Bennet, I have been searching everywhere for you. Lady Catherine requires your presence. Immediately, if you please, miss."

Icy fingers clutched Elizabeth's heart. "Whatever for? Has there been an express from Longbourn or London? Or has something occurred at Hunsford?"

"I have not been made privy to that information, miss."

In a gesture of proper respect, Mr Darcy offered his arm and seemed intent on escorting her to his aunt. "If I may, Miss Bennet?"

She flinched. "There is no need, sir." Glancing at his countenance, she descried the indisputable hurt caused by her reluctance.

Poorly done, Lizzy. Do not be so spiteful. Thanking him and gingerly placing her hand upon his sleeve, Elizabeth thought she might never again be in charity with not only Mr Darcy but with herself.

The footman trailed behind as they headed down the frost-covered woodland path and into the park. Although Mr Darcy walked with long, confident strides, Elizabeth easily kept pace, anxious about the tidings awaiting her.

Both silent as the grave, she fancied that Mr Darcy, he of the furrowed brow and undue interest in the hawthorn hedges—*as prickly as the man himself*—was as discomfited in her company as she remained in his.

Discourse about the item in her pocket was avoided, but the letter practically burnt a hole there, so afire was her curiosity to know its subject. She feared that in addition to information pertaining to Mr Wickham it might contain a further appeal for her hand.

In his presence, she could not help but recall Mr Darcy's fervent declaration from the previous evening. It had started so beautifully. *'You must allow me to tell you how ardently I admire and love you.'* Who would not be affected by such an avowal? Had he stopped there, she would not have responded so harshly or have regrets that morning about the petulance and acrimony she had hurled at him. Despite the chilly air and the ice gripping her heart, a warm flush overspread Elizabeth's body, and a dreadful embarrassment radiated down her arm to where her gloved hand rested upon the sleeve of the man who claimed he loved her.

But he could not long occupy her thoughts, for alarming presentiments of disaster began running pell-mell through her mind. Lady Catherine's summons could only mean she had learnt of some calamity or of her nephew's proposal. After all, Miss de Bourgh was supposedly promised to him.

They walked through the park and into the gardens, each step bringing Elizabeth closer to what surely would bring either sorrow or her ladyship's wrath. Seeking suspension of anxiety, she prayed for the latter. But if it was about the proposal, why should she be reprimanded and held accountable for an unexpected and unwanted offer? Why must she suffer the consequences of another person's folly?

Will Mr Darcy find himself in the hateful position of being obliged to remain by my side and answer for his transgression?

Chapter Three

As they walked on, Darcy fervently prayed no ill tidings from Longbourn awaited Elizabeth, and he contemplated other possibilities for the summons.

Could his aunt have learnt of his proposal? And if so, might she hold another person accountable? The weight of Atlas's celestial sphere shifted from his shoulders, only to settle upon his chest.

He would not allow Elizabeth to suffer ill consequences from what could only be called his own foolhardiness. By her side he would stand, defending the young lady against any and all of Lady Catherine's accusations. Taking root in his brain, those imminent and unfair charges bloomed in vivid, mortifying detail—his aunt pointing the finger of blame at Elizabeth, insisting her arts and allurements, in an instant of passion, had drawn him in, making him forget himself and everything he owed his family, namely Miss Anne de Bourgh. *What a heap of absurdities.*

But not all of it was absurd. Elizabeth's allurements *had* drawn him like metal filings to a mighty magnet. Not only powerfully attractive, she utterly fascinated him. And he would wager his last guinea that she wielded no artful wiles. Honest to a fault, she had had no qualms about pointing out *his* faults.

Frowning, Darcy nearly stopped in his tracks.

My faults. They may be heavy, indeed. Had Elizabeth the right of it? Was he arrogant, conceited, and selfish? Was he disdainful of others' feelings? He wished he had voiced his concerns to Fitzwilliam while he had the chance. Whether he welcomed it or not, his cousin would have delivered both the unvarnished truth and invaluable counsel.

All acrimony he had directed towards Elizabeth gradually turned his own way. *My proposal was an abomination.*

Falling in love was a novel and utterly painful experience, and as he passed the prickly hedges stretching up and down the lane, he gave a passing thought to the belief that hawthorn was purported to heal a broken heart. But as a man of education and intelligence, Darcy put faith in science, not myths, superstitions, or false hopes. The woman with whom he had wanted to spend the rest of his life had rejected him, and that was the end of it.

Unbidden, his father's voice intruded upon his thoughts. *'A gentleman does not offend a lady's sensibilities.'* That lesson had been inculcated in him, and Darcy felt duly ashamed. The previous evening, by detailing feelings other than those of the heart, he had offended and insulted an exemplary lady, the woman he purported to love. Why had he spoken of her inferiority and of family obstacles?

I even might have uttered the word degradation and something about my scruples. Damn. What scruples? At the rate his heavy heart kept sinking, it would soon be in his boots.

Within minutes in a most abrupt and precipitate manner, his relations' palatial residence loomed ahead of him. So preoccupied had he been, brooding the entire time it took to reach the manor, that he had not spoken a word to the precious creature by his side. *Ungallant swine!* It mattered not. She obviously took greater delight in their surroundings than in his company.

"Well," he said, climbing the front steps, "here we are." *What a talent I possess for enlightening conversation!*

A loud rumble erupted beside him, and a dainty gloved palm quickly covered the lady's obviously empty stomach. "I beg your pardon, sir. By now, I have missed breakfast at the parsonage. I told Mrs Collins I would take only a short walk in the grove." In a manner arousing Darcy's sympathy, she added, "As was my wont."

His heart landed in his boots, leaving his chest hollow. Around the lump in his throat, he said, "As *was* your wont. This morning, to avoid me, you took to the woods and—"

The front door opened, and a footman collected their coats. Before relinquishing her pelisse, Elizabeth surreptitiously slipped Darcy's letter from that pocket into one in the folds of her gown. That she was so protective of it and of her reputation gave him a sense of relief and not inconsiderable guilt.

Informed that Lady Catherine and Anne awaited Elizabeth in the morning room, Darcy offered his arm, and they followed the footman through an ante-chamber to where his aunt, cousin, and Mrs Jenkinson sat.

A good blaze sizzled in the white marble fireplace, making the east-facing parlour comfortably warm. With its tasteful paper-hangings, tapestries, and Brussels-weave carpets, it was less extravagantly showy than the more formal drawing room.

When Darcy did not immediately move away, Elizabeth looked out of the corner of her eye at him. "Until I know my aunt's business with you," he whispered, "I shall not leave your side." At that assertion, she appeared at once all perplexity and vexation.

"Darcy, you may leave us." Heavy with rings, Lady Catherine's fingers waggled at him in dismissal.

No, he would not be flicked away like a gnat. After greeting the others, seating their guest, and requesting tea and toasted muffins, Darcy sank into the matching Gillows tub chair nearest Elizabeth and gave his aunt a defiant look.

Pretending to have taken no notice of his open resistance, Lady Catherine turned to her visitor. "Now then, Miss Bennet, I was seriously displeased to learn that you—"

Prepared to jump to the young lady's defence, Darcy

shifted to the edge of his seat and leant forwards, twisting his signet ring.

Her ladyship's narrowed eyes locked on him. "If you insist on remaining here, you will cease fidgeting at once, Darcy! Come over here, and sit on the sofa beside Anne, where you belong."

Belong? Because the better part of valour is discretion, Darcy reluctantly moved across the room and sat as directed. From that vantage point, he noticed that the four pastoral de Bourgh tapestries—one for each season—seemed duller than he remembered. He was about to ask his cousin's opinion of them when her ladyship spoke again.

"As I was saying, Miss Bennet, I was seriously displeased to learn you would leave before my daughter's ball. It is a pity Miss Lucas became inconveniently homesick after only a se'nnight and departed with Sir William, but I knew *you* could not possibly care to leave us so soon. To that end, I took it upon myself to write to your mother, insisting you be permitted to remain a while longer. Mrs Collins will be very glad of your company, I am sure."

Darcy's head snapped to Elizabeth's flushed face and widened eyes as she said, "I am much obliged to your ladyship, but with all due respect, I really must leave on the eighteenth. My uncle is to send his manservant for me on that date, and my sister and relations will be awaiting my arrival in town."

"You seem quite out of humour this morning, but it is within my means to occasion a most delightful reanimation of such downcast spirits." Holding up a sheet of paper, Lady Catherine employed a lorgnette to peruse it. "Your mother replied saying she has no objection to your staying and that Mr Bennet will certainly agree once she advises him to do so. Of course, daughters never are of much consequence to a father. Indeed, all your family and relations can spare you until after Anne's celebration."

"You are all kindness, madam." Elizabeth's over-bright eyes darted towards Darcy. "But I must abide by my original plan."

Because of me, she will not accede. Blast. I know how much she enjoys dancing.

"Not so hasty, if you please." Her ladyship's bejewelled fingers reached for something on a silver salver. "Your mother's reply included correspondence addressed to yourself. Nephew, make yourself useful and pass this to Miss Bennet."

Darcy did so, and standing before the young lady, he made two observations. She cringed while accepting a second letter from his hand, and one of her bootlaces was untied. Without a second thought, he dropped to a knee. "Please," he said, pointing to Elizabeth's boot, "allow me."

"What are you about now? Get up off the floor at once, Darcy! Heaven and earth! You resemble a sentimental noddy on bended knee like that. Such respect should be reserved for dear Anne."

I did not hear that. Once the bootlace was retied and secured with a tight double knot, Darcy stood and studied

Elizabeth's mien. Perceiving the mortification in her eyes, he whispered, "I am so very sorry." Returning to his cousin's side, he wondered for what exactly he had just apologised.

A maid arrived with the requested tea tray, and the serving and partaking of refreshments occupied everyone until Lady Catherine indicated Elizabeth should attend to her mother's reply.

What seemed to be a single sheet of paper was then opened, read, slowly refolded, and added to the other letter in her pocket. Lifting her eyes to gaze longingly towards the door, she softly said, "It is as you say, Lady Catherine. My family can spare me until after the ball, and my uncle is being informed of the change in plans." Her chin lifted, and she spoke with determination. "However, I cannot possibly impose upon Mr and Mrs Collins."

"What nonsense! With *my* approbation, neither you nor the Collinses can have any objection whatsoever."

Another voice, a gentler one, spoke up. "And if the rector and his wife are unable to accommodate you, you are welcome to be *my* guest here at Rosings." With varying degrees of surprise, Lady Catherine, Darcy, Elizabeth, and Mrs Jenkinson turned to look upon Anne. "What? We have adequate room for one more houseguest, and as my mother said, there can be no reason for your going so soon. Please, Miss Bennet, say you will stay for my celebratory ball. We shall have a grand time, I assure you."

In such close proximity to his cousin, Darcy heard her

next words, though she spoke under her breath. "If you enjoy surprises, that is."

The look of dread on Elizabeth's face rent Darcy's heart. *To have coerced her into such a position! The poor dear has no choice but to accept the invitation, yet neither of us wishes to be forced into one another's company.*

Chapter Four

Marching away from Rosings towards Hunsford, Elizabeth was impervious to the chill in the air. Vigorous activity and the vexations of life kept her blood heated. Such was her undignified stride that the long-legged footman—whom Lady Catherine had insisted accompany her—dog-trotted to keep pace. Exasperated thoughts knew no moderation, particularly regarding Mr Darcy, that gentleman's meddlesome aunt, and her own marriage-minded mother.

I shall take to my grave the fact that Mama suggested I somehow inveigle an invitation to Miss de Bourgh's ball for all my sisters.

Just as Elizabeth, with considerable exaggeration and not a little self-pity, wondered whether her circumstance could possibly become any more wretched, icy pellets with a hard, sugary consistency began pelting her face and forming sloppy conditions underfoot. Slipping and sliding, she grumbled to herself for half a mile. *Misery, thy name is spring sleet.*

Not customarily formed for prolonged ill-humour, upon arrival at the parsonage, Elizabeth spent an inordinate amount of time struggling to untie a wet bootlace with chilled fingers. *Botheration!* It was the same one Mr Darcy had secured with such a knot as would have defeated a strong, seasoned seaman.

After requesting tea, she settled, warm and dry, upon a small sofa beside the fire. Just as she broke the seal on the gentleman's letter, Molly entered balancing a tea service complete with toasted, buttery muffins and damson preserves. The maid was thanked, and Elizabeth was left alone to tuck into a second breakfast.

Mrs Collins soon ducked her head round the door jamb. "I shall join you in a moment, Eliza."

While awaiting her friend, Elizabeth consigned the letter to her pocket again and turned her thoughts to Miss de Bourgh's forthcoming celebration. Under ordinary circumstances, the anticipation of a private ball would have filled her with eager expectations of pleasure. *But Mr Darcy will be there. And my cousin with his clumsy feet and inability to move separate parts of his body together gracefully.*

A line from her mother's letter came to mind. *'Your father says that by staying longer, you will have time to further observe the follies and foibles of Mr Collins and his patroness.'*

In comparison to the long-suffering Mrs Collins and Miss de Bourgh, Elizabeth admitted her lot in life was not so very wretched. After all, she would have to remain in Kent only three additional days.

I shall persevere...even if it kills me. I simply shall avoid seeing Mr Darcy until the night of the ball. And Lady Catherine had the right of it. Dear Charlotte cannot object to my staying a little longer. But how awkward I shall feel making such a request.

The lady of the house then joined her on the sofa and poured herself a cup of tea. "You had an extraordinarily long walk in the cold this morning. I trust your outing helped alleviate whatever ailed you last night and earlier today." It was more question than statement. "Still, you seem out of sorts."

Not even to her dear friend would Elizabeth divulge what had transpired the previous evening in that very room. Surely Charlotte would think her a simpleton for refusing a gentleman of such consequence. It had taken her own mother an entire se'nnight to forgive her for refusing Mr Collins.

Mama must never know that not only our cousin but another of the men invited to Miss de Bourgh's ball made me a marriage offer and was rejected. For an instant, Elizabeth felt like the most selfish, ungrateful daughter on the face of the earth, but she refused to be sacrificed on the altar of her mother's ambition.

"I find myself most awkwardly circumstanced this morning, Charlotte, and I fear what I am about to say will result in mutual embarrassment." With all mention of Mr Darcy's involvement carefully omitted, a compendious history was given of what had transpired at Rosings.

"The audacity of her! Such presumption was beyond belief." Drawing in slow, steady breaths, Elizabeth stilled her restless hands upon her lap. "What business had she going behind my back and writing to my parents with no regard whatsoever for my wishes? And to prevail upon *you* to accommodate me beyond my scheduled departure is unconscionable. Wretched woman! I do not wish to be a burden but find myself obliged to impose upon your hospitality a little longer."

Charlotte had listened to Elizabeth's litany of complaints with earnest attention. "Lady Catherine admires you—almost as much as Mr Darcy does—though neither of them ever would admit such. Her ladyship would not have gone to such trouble for someone of whom she disapproves. And truly, your remaining is no imposition at all. I am happy to have you here with me. You know I value your friendship beyond that of any other person." She gave her friend's shoulder a gentle nudge.

The gesture was returned. "I have no doubt of your warm regard, Charlotte. Thank you."

It had taken Elizabeth quite some time before becoming reconciled to the November engagement and January marriage of Mr Collins and the then Miss Lucas. Esteem for her friend had sunk under the weight of disappointment and disapproval, and there had existed between the two a restraint. Absence, however, had increased Elizabeth's desire to see Charlotte and even weakened her disgust of the woman's husband. It saddened her to suspect the couple shared no grand passion. Had her cousin ever spoken of how much he admired and loved his wife? *Will anyone ever again speak such ardent words to me?*

Those thoughts were interrupted by Molly who informed them Mr Chapman, a parishioner, was at the door beseeching Mr and Mrs Collins to attend his dying wife. Elizabeth considered accompanying them, but although she was not insensible of their plight, she was unknown to the Chapmans and would be neither welcome nor helpful at such a time.

Instead, she went to her bedchamber where the fire of curiosity could be extinguished in privacy. Once seated upon the edge of the bed, she opened Mr Darcy's letter and read it through twice in its entirety and thrice those sections regarding Mr Bingley and Jane as well as Mr Wickham and Miss Darcy. With each reading, the written words caused outrage, sorrow, and pain of the heart. Afflicted by a coalescence of feelings, she tossed the pages aside and paced the small room in trembling wretchedness.

The clanging and clattering of pots and plates from the kitchen could not drown out the clamour in her mind—a jumble of ire, mortification, and commiseration. Fairly vibrating with it, she could scarcely contain her animosity towards Mr Darcy's obtuse defence of his action against her dearest sister and the disdain he felt for the rest of her family.

Then there was the matter of how gravely disloyal the despicable Mr Wickham had been to the Darcys. How mortifying it was for Elizabeth to realise she, too, had been endowed with susceptible naiveté and had courted prejudice and ignorance.

Duly ashamed of her mistaken first impressions of the two men, Elizabeth gave an anguished cry and dashed away tears of frustration with herself and of sympathy for Miss Darcy. How could she possibly face the girl's brother again with any degree of equanimity?

Prone then upon the bed, she chastised herself over and over again. *Since the very beginning of my acquaintance with Mr Darcy and Mr Wickham, I drove away all reason. Stupid girl.*

Tears soaked her pillow, but after much reflection and self-reproach, she admitted Mr Darcy's explanations vindicated a portion of *his* insufferable behaviour but not her own.

Chapter Five

Saturday, April 11

Having been informed she was 'obtuse'—not to mention 'mad'—Anne vigorously exerted herself to repel her cousin's ill-natured aspersions. Although Darcy was less than ten years her senior, he had become an insufferably dull, pompous, overbearing brute. *Albeit a brute I cannot help but hold in high regard.*

Lady Catherine always claimed she and Lady Anne Darcy had planned a union between the two cousins while they were in their cradles. Anne laughed to herself, picturing Pemberley's heir, tall even at that young age, squeezed into an infant's cradle. *Such balderdash! Why, Darcy was a lad of nearly seven when I was born. The sisters might have agreed that it would be advantageously pleasing if Darcy and I decided to wed, but that will not happen.*

The cousins' latest difference of opinion had begun half

an hour earlier when Darcy exited the library and espied Anne in the hall where she donned her gloves—the soft tan ones embroidered with her monogram. Darcy had given her those gloves, and she always and only wore them while driving.

"Where are you going," he asked.

Though Anne thought it should be obvious and none of his business, she said, "Out." Tucking her book and riding whip under one arm, she waggled eight kid-clad fingers in front of his face. "In my phaeton."

"*You* are venturing out in this cold? There was sleet earlier, Anne. And you are not going alone, are you? Take either Mrs Jenkinson or your lady's maid with you."

"The former is asleep in her chair, snoring and drooling, and the latter cannot be spared. At present, Dubois is putting finishing enhancements on my full-dress gown."

Anne flattered herself in thinking she possessed a degree of captivating deceit, particularly when adding her own little embellishments, such as the snoring and drooling detail.

Dear old Mrs Jenkinson! I should not ridicule the fine lady who superintended my education and is supposed to be available at all hours to satisfy my needs and maintain propriety. Still, Anne appreciated how doting her companion was and how protective she was of her charge's comfort.

Darcy beckoned a footman and requested his own coat, scarf, hat, and gloves be fetched. "*I* shall accompany you."

You would have to kill me first. "I thank you, but no. As they say, 'One's too few, three too many'."

Crossing his arms, Darcy said, "You are being either evasive, deliberately obtuse, or both. Pray tell *who* will attend you?"

Lifting heels off the floor and stretching her neck, Anne tried to gain an inch or two. Although her mother was a tall woman, her father had been rather squat, and Darcy towered above her.

"I shall be with Mr Brinton." Her cousin's face grew livid at that. *See what happens when one tells the truth?*

"Brinton? *Brinton!* Are you completely mad?"

"Of course not. I simply said his name to see how you would react." It was no lie. "If you must know, Gilchrist promised to show me where the wild cherry trees may be found." Again, no lie. "I want to press some of their frothy, delicate blossoms in my Flora." Anne held up the book, glad she had thought to bring it along, though she had no real interest in using it. As for what she planned to do afterwards, she did not feel it necessary to disclose such information. It was none of Darcy's business.

Besides, why would it be 'mad' to go for a drive with Laurence Brinton but quite acceptable to do so with Iain Gilchrist?

Obviously, Anne knew why. One was an eligible gentleman bachelor and an infamous flirt. The other was a loyal servant, and she, a wealthy, innocent damsel, was his employer.

It was with gentle persuasion and much acuity that Anne eventually softened her cousin into complaisance. She first, however, had to agree Darcy could accompany her as far as Gilchrist's cottage—just beyond the glass-roofed structures where tender plants were raised and exotic ones protected.

And that was where, a quarter of an hour later, they encountered her master gardener. Anne already considered Iain Gilchrist to be in her employ because Lady Catherine would control Rosings for only another nine days.

The Scotsman, in Anne's opinion, was a dark-haired Adonis upon whom nature had bestowed more than his fair share of attractiveness. Tall and well-formed like the plants in one of the hothouses, he was exotically handsome. His face, while bronzed, was unlined for he still was a relatively young man. Customarily, he wore a myrtle-green coat, pristine shirt and cravat, nankeen inexpressibles, and boots that looked like Hessians—far too fashionable for a mere gardener. Because he wore gloves while working, his fingernails were spotless, and he smelt of earth, dried herbs, and greenery. Anne's only complaint was that, at certain times, he spoke with a perplexing Highland Scottish burr.

When the cousins greeted Gilchrist outside the orangery, the gardener doffed his cap and bid them good morning.

Anne had not realised she was staring at the well-favoured fellow until Darcy's throat was cleared with exaggeration. Once upon a time, she had been infatuated with Gilchrist. *But a gentlewoman and a gardener! Can you imagine the scandal?* Admittedly, she still felt great affection for the man, and the regard was mutual. However, never would she unscrupulously control or influence someone in her employ. *He is a willing partner in my—our—scheme.*

After exchanging a few civilities, Darcy said to Gilchrist, "Please ensure Miss de Bourgh is not kept over-long in this frigid air." With that, he took his leave of Anne and her gardener.

Later, near the woodland, Anne sat in her phaeton while her ponies stamped and snorted. Her toes and fingertips were freezing, her entire body shivered, and she held a handkerchief to her nose while Gilchrist plucked unwanted wild cherry blossoms for her.

Soon though, she knew they both would be warm and cosy enough, albeit not in either her grand manor or the gardener's sweet little cottage. Instead, they would cut across the woods and onto the road, all the way to Rara Avis for a brief call.

Teasingly referring to her as milady, Gilchrist passed Anne the delicate white flowers, and she laughed with him while carelessly placing the blossoms between pages in the middle of her Flora. They were the only plants therein, but she supposed she would have to collect more specimens to satisfy her mother and cynical cousin.

Nearly giddy with ebullience and anticipation, she urged her ponies to move along at a lively trot while Gilchrist held onto his cap.

Rara Avis and its young master are like nothing else and no one I have ever known. Which is not saying much. Rarely do I make or receive calls.

Brinton's home, though seldom was he in residence

there, was a trove of treasures from faraway lands. It was alive with music and with plants and birds and knick-knacks not native to England's shores.

In that marvellous manor and on those beautiful grounds, Anne felt as though she *was* exploring and experiencing the world. On that estate, she felt *alive,* never sullen or in ill health.

And she would trade Rosings Park for Rara Avis in a heartbeat.

Chapter Six

The air remained crisp, more mid-winter than April. Rare sightings of sunlight amongst clouds were so unexpected and inviting that after leaving Anne in Gilchrist's care, Darcy continued rambling. He had no particular destination in mind, but his feet—*the traitors*—led him to a certain young lady's favourite haunt at the edge of the park, a grove which no one but Elizabeth herself seemed to value.

In the distance, Hunsford's church bell tolled six times, marking the death of a parishioner. Three strokes, twice. An adult female. Removing his hat, Darcy bowed his head and said a prayer for the soul of the departed woman. The knell then sounded one stroke for each year of her life. *Twenty-nine. Not much older than I. Too young.*

Continuing through the grove, he considered retreating when Elizabeth, advancing in his direction, was spotted through the trees. Fearing she might turn away upon descrying him, he stepped forwards and spoke her name. Her heightened colour, Darcy supposed, resulted from the perverseness of another encounter with him. *Or might I entertain the notion that, after reading my letter, she has changed her mind and has thrown herself in my way? By George, I truly am an arrogant lout.* No doubt, her rosy bloom was from being out and about on that hibernal morn.

"We meet again, Miss Bennet."

As she neared and curtseyed, he noted that although her cheeks were rosy, her eyes did not appear at all brightened by the exercise. In fact, they looked swollen, like his sister's after a bout of weeping, and he wondered whether it was the consequence of having read his letter. Darcy nearly fell to his knees.

"What is it?" he asked, dreading her answer. "What has happened? Are you unwell?"

With the sort of civility he envied, she replied, "I am well, thank you." Only after turning her face skywards did she smile. "It is a fine day for a walk, albeit chilly. One could hardly complain of being incommoded by the heat thus far this spring. The sun's return, although weak, is most heartily welcome." Elizabeth's puffy, red-rimmed eyes studied the surrounding park. "During my sojourn here, I had hoped to see some of Kent's gardens in bloom, but I fear prolonged frost will severely delay planting or destroy whatever has been sown already."

Darcy could converse eloquently and effortlessly with a marquess or a duchess, even royalty, but he found it difficult to do so with Elizabeth. Weather and agriculture, though, were subjects he could discuss with ease.

"I believe this is the coldest spring we have had since ninety-nine. So, yes, the harvesting of crops may be late this year and of a low yield. As for blooms, although Rosings Park's gardens are rather too formal for my taste, I wish you could see the flowers in all their splendour. In Kent, gardens are as common as people are in London." The look on her face gave him pause. *What? What did I say?*

"Do you mean common as in vulgar—with a lack of refinement and taste?"

"No." He heaved a sigh. "I meant common as in prevalent." His explanation seemed to appease her, for she no longer scowled. In a gesture indicating the entire park, Darcy added, "These seventeen acres are maintained by a battalion of gardeners and labourers overseen by Gilchrist, a master gardener. Lady Catherine disparages the man as having little sense because he has yet to solicit her own, as she calls it, *gardening proficiency*."

The smile Elizabeth offered was as weak as the sunlight, but it encouraged him to continue, and he pointed southwards. "The eccentric owner of the neighbouring estate was in the Highlands several years ago acquiring plants native to that region, such as bog myrtle, heathers, and such. While there, he hired Iain Gilchrist, a much renowned horticulturist, for Rara Avis. In Gilchrist's own words, he was 'uprooted from his Scottish home and planted in Kent'. As you may know, Scots are preferred master gardeners, for they have the best training. I employ one myself at Pemberley."

"Does Gilchrist work for both Rara Avis and Rosings?"

Why did I broach this subject? I certainly shall not be mentioning the rumours to her or to any lady. "No, only the latter. While I was here last Easter, Gilchrist came to me asking for a position at Rosings, claiming he was intrigued by the possibilities a larger estate offered. He came with excellent references. With good reason, Lady Catherine does not care for the young gentleman who inherited Rara Avis. He is too free-spirited for her liking. So initially at least, she was proud that Rosings Park's grandeur lured Gilchrist away from Mr Brinton."

Having struck upon a befitting change of subject, Darcy said, "Of late, my cousin Anne has taken a keen interest in botany, particularly the flora hereabouts. As we speak, she is being assisted by Gilchrist in putting together an herbarium, or a Flora, as she calls it."

"You mentioned hiring Rosings Park's head gardener, and it made me realise you must be a very capable but busy gentleman, what with the overseeing of your own grand estate, the assistance you gave Mr Bingley at Netherfield, and tending to matters here for your aunt and cousin. You take on a great deal of responsibility, sir."

"It certainly keeps me out of trouble." Pleased to have Elizabeth's undivided attention, he smiled and added, "Well, *mostly*."

"How are you able to spend so much time away from Pemberley?"

"I employ a competent steward, a matchless housekeeper, responsible groundsmen, and as I said, a superb master gardener. He and his under-gardeners work long hours caring for the archery, cricket, and bowling lawns as well as maintaining proper temperatures in the conservatory and orangery. We also hire, as necessary, myriad seasonal labourers to tend the grounds and orchards."

Darcy thought that moment might be an auspicious opportunity to demonstrate an interest in her relations. "Speaking of working the land, do you not have an uncle who is a gardener? I seem to recall Miss Bingley mentioning such."

Why is she rubbing her brow? Has she a headache? Blast. Narrowed eyes and the pressing together of her lips did not bode well for him.

Planting her fists on her hips, Elizabeth turned blazing eyes upon him. "No, I do not. However, I do have an uncle, aunt, and four cousins whose surname is Gardiner. G-A-R-D-I-N-E-R."

The spelling was done with painful slowness, as though Darcy was dim-witted. Why had he not shown an interest in those who were most important to her? Why had he been unwilling to associate with the people she held dear?

"I am deeply ashamed, and I apologise for being presumptuous. Your relations deserve respect."

"I hope you are not begging forgiveness on behalf of Miss Bingley, sir. You are not to blame for her misinformation."

"True. But I have made numerous blunders myself, abominably stupid ones, where you and your loved ones are concerned. For those faults, I beg your pardon."

Given absolution, Darcy thought Elizabeth the most generous soul of his acquaintance, but being in her charming company after a failed proposal was sweet torture. Her presence threw him into not only contrary feelings of disquiet and delight but determination. A resolution was formed. He would change for the better, not only in the hope of improving her opinion of him but because it was the honourable thing to do. He would be patient and perhaps, God willing, the woman he loved would grow to think better of him.

Hugging herself, Elizabeth rubbed her upper arms. "Shall we walk? 'Tis chilly standing here."

They entered the park's bisecting avenue that over the years the sun had bleached to a stark whiteness. Crunching seashells beneath his boots, Darcy rattled away about the whelks, cockles, and limpets that had come from a bay bordering Margate. *Why am I babbling about marine mollusks? Why are we even speaking of this when there is a letter to discuss?*

"You once hinted that I am of a taciturn disposition, unwilling to speak. But no longer can I hesitate to raise the matter of my letter, which I wish had never been penned. Please tell me you burnt the wretched thing." Darcy glanced her way, but she made no response. "My purpose in writing was to warn you about Mr Wickham. I also hoped, and still do, it might make you think better of me. However, I fear my explanations and certain wording therein may have caused you pain." He longed to see her expression, but the pretty bonnet she wore obstructed his view.

She stopped walking, scuffing the toe of her boot against washed-out seashells. "Upon initial perusal yesterday, I wanted to rip your letter to shreds." Looking him in the eye she added, "Now I treasure it."

Darcy sucked in a breath. "*Treasure* it? I rather imagined you might have wanted to rip *me* to shreds after reading such bitterness. Please say you might one day forgive me."

"For which of your transgressions do you now seek forgiveness, sir? Your treatment of Jane specifically or the way you behaved towards my family, friends, and neighbours? Had I not read your letter, I would have added Mr Wickham to that list." The soft leather of Elizabeth's gloves strained against knuckles as her hands formed into fists. "Needless to say, the scoundrel has lost my esteem."

The smile she then offered was a sad sort of one. "I cherish the trust you have shown by relating your dear sister's misfortune. You may count on my discretion." Gesturing towards the grove, she said, "Shall we make another circuit of the park?"

Darcy agreed with brisk readiness. The sort of unreserved, uninterrupted, and intimate communication she seemed willing to share with him was nothing short of his heart's desire.

Chapter Seven

All sense of time was lost to her as Elizabeth walked and talked with Mr Darcy, her gloved palm curled round his arm.

Hesitantly at first, the gentleman spoke of his sister, his parents, and his upbringing. "My father instilled in me the importance of honesty, of self-command, and of strong moral principles. I have strived to live up to his expectations."

"You mention honesty." Elizabeth's curiosity would not be conquered. Her dignity and vanity demanded satisfaction. "So, at the Meryton assembly, were you being truthful when you said I was not handsome enough to tempt you? If so, why would you have wished to make me your wife? Or was it all a scurrilous falsehood?" It had been something of a scandal throughout Longbourn village and Meryton, but that had been her own fault for spreading word of the insult.

Mr Darcy's voice lost much of its power. "There is no adequate excuse for that callous remark, but I did not know you when it was uttered. I barely glanced at you or anyone that night." He touched the fingers resting upon his sleeve and indicated they should stop walking. Turning, he caught her eye. "The truth, madam, is that you—"

The look he bestowed upon her made Elizabeth blush.

"The truth is that the better I came to know you, the more your beauty, like a rosebud, blossomed before my eyes. It is greater than the sum of its parts."

"My *parts?*"

"I mean your appeal is a combination of—" He seemed to struggle for a compliment. "What shall I call it? Your, um—"

"You must mean my *je ne sais quoi,* for I certainly do not know what you mean." She did, but a vindictive part of her wanted him to squirm. Though less out of favour, he was still in her black books.

The gentleman's words spilled forth in a rush. "I mean your appeal is a combination of intelligence, compassion, and loyalty. I even admire your defence of the supposedly downtrodden, even when they do not deserve it. And I admit I am strangely attracted to your temerity. Mostly, though, it is your exuberance. Even here and now, despite the enmity you feel towards me, your enjoyment of life shines through like the sun through these clouds. You, I think, are not formed for petulance. Unlike me, your manners have all the recommendations of ease, good humour, and unaffectedness. I wish—for your own sake and for that of others—that I had your amiability amongst company. And how I dearly wish I could undo all my past mistakes."

Slowing his speech, he seemed intent on articulation. "I once told you that I have not that talent you possess of conversing easily with strangers. I cannot appear interested in their concerns, as I often see you do so admirably."

When he touched on the matter of Wickham and Miss Darcy, Elizabeth asked thoughtful questions and expressed genuine concern for his sister and for him, and she was thanked for it.

"Mr Darcy, you know I never hesitate to express pert opinions. Now that I comprehend your circumstances, it is easier to be forthright with you, a gentleman I previously held in contempt and treated with irreverence. How could I be less than completely frank when you were so brutally candid in your revealing letter? Your entrusting me with Miss Darcy's secret speaks of great faith in my discretion. If I am to be honest—not only with you but with myself—your candour and trust are earning you a claim on my good will."

"I am very glad to hear it." He smiled then, quite handsomely, but it faded into a frown as he mentioned his abysmal offer of marriage.

Remorseful about her response to that proposal, Elizabeth clasped her hands in front of her and studied them, not him. *Such blunders! Such blindness of head and heart!*

"I utterly misconducted myself that evening, sir, and

my conscience will not acquit me." A sting formed in her eyes as they watered not from cold but from shame.

She raised her chin to look him in the eye. "I did not behave in a ladylike manner." Her voice cracked, and a tear fell unheeded. "How despicably I acted, and how aggrieved you must have felt!" A sob broke free. "Will you ever find it in your heart to forgive the harsh words I spoke?"

"Hush now." Mr Darcy stepped closer and gently dabbed her cheek with a pristine handkerchief. "Every word you just said, I repeat back to you." He smiled. "With the exception of *ladylike*. We both know *I* did not behave in a gentlemanlike manner. So, let us agree to absolve one another, and let us look not backwards but towards the future."

Sniffling and smiling, Elizabeth nodded her head in hearty agreement.

Of Mr Bingley's leaving Netherfield they spoke at length. To Elizabeth, it was evident her elder sister was very much in love with Mr Darcy's friend, but she admitted it was not likely to be discovered by others.

"Charlotte told me that being so very guarded would be disadvantageous, and if Jane concealed her affection from the object of it, she might lose the opportunity of fixing him."

Mr Darcy nodded his understanding. "I know a foolish man, blinded by pride, who mistook a lady's assurance of manner for coquetry. He unknowingly concealed his burgeoning love from her—the most worthy of women—

and thereby lost any opportunity of ever securing her affection. Were he not already desolate, he should be tarred, feathered, and pilloried." With her pensive regard fixed upon his face, he asked whether her expression was one of solicitude or of pity. "The gentleman would not want your sympathy, madam. He still wishes to secure the young lady's affection."

Oh dear! Several retorts made it as far as the tip of Elizabeth's tongue but remained unvoiced.

By unspoken agreement, they walked on in awkward silence. When a few minutes had elapsed, Mr Darcy promised to send Mr Bingley back to her sister.

"It was very badly done of me to have interfered as I did, poking my nose in where it had no business."

"What of my family, sir? Have you changed your stance about them? I might argue that you as a gentleman and I as a gentleman's daughter are equals. But the truth is that you are infinitely Jane's and my superior in consequence and wealth."

"True, but that is not so for Bingley. He is not of the gentry. Your family holds higher standing, though your father's wealth falls far short of my friend's. At any rate..." Mr Darcy paused until she looked him in the eye. "None of that should matter a jot when a man has fallen in love."

When a man has fallen in love. A blush overspread Elizabeth's cheeks, and a tingle shot down her spine as she turned away. Without confirmation, she sensed the gentleman's heated, penetrating gaze fixed upon her profile.

Despite her refusal of his marriage offer, it was increasingly evident he remained attached to her.

It was all too much. She needed time to think. "Mr Darcy, what is the hour? How long have we been walking?"

He consulted his pocket watch. "A quarter of eleven. Are you fatigued or in need of sustenance?"

Elizabeth admitted she had, once again, not yet eaten breakfast. "I must go, but I very much enjoyed our conversation." She curtseyed. "Good day, sir."

"I shall escort you to the parsonage."

The authority with which he had spoken rankled. "Whatever for? I am perfectly accustomed to walking hereabouts unaccompanied and have been doing so off and on for a month now. Besides, have you forgotten my answer from the other evening? We may have put aside our differences and are learning to be civil towards one another, but you are not responsible for my welfare."

The instant the words were out of Elizabeth's mouth, she wished them unsaid. Mr Darcy's crestfallen mien caused her a degree of shame. *Of course, a true gentleman* would *consider himself responsible.*

Just then, there came such a cacophony of rattles, squeaks, and the clatter of hooves on gravel that both of them turned in the direction of the lane.

"That is Anne's phaeton approaching with undue speed," said Mr Darcy. "And from the wrong direction. She was to confer with Gilchrist about her herbarium, then directly return home. Where the dickens has she been all this time?" He apologised for the outburst but took no pains to conceal his vexation and concern.

"Make haste then, sir, and ascertain Miss de Bourgh's welfare. I shall pray there is no need for such apprehension."

Chapter Eight

Respecting Elizabeth's wishes, Darcy bid her a good day and let her go, but as he watched her walk away, something she had said weighed heavily on his thoughts. *'You are not responsible for my welfare.' Yes, thank you for reminding me that this heart of mine belongs to someone who does not want it.*

Darcy recollected himself before he could be completely overtaken by sentiment, and although he was not directly responsible for Anne's welfare either, he set off after her, anxious about what might have delayed his cousin's return from the outing with Gilchrist. Hoping to catch her before she reached the manor, he hastened towards the carriage house, a two-storey structure housing the barouche, chaise, phaeton, and Darcy's own coach. Above were living quarters for the coachman, grooms, and stable hands. Horses were accommodated in the nearby barn.

He espied her between those two buildings. Anne saw him, he knew she did, but she pretended she had not and strode towards the house at an amazingly quick pace.

Close behind, Darcy raised his voice. "Anne! Where have you been?"

"Not now, Cousin." Tucking something beneath one arm and hitching up her skirts, she broke into a run, shouting over her shoulder. "It is freezing cold, and I am rather late. Her ladyship will have my guts for garters."

Darcy took chase across the lawns, hard on her heels, until he reached her. "How prodigiously eloquent you have become of late. When did you learn to run like that, and from whence has all this unexpected vitality sprung?" His cousin was quite an altered creature since last he had visited Rosings, and he truly was glad that she no longer appeared quite so pale and sickly. "I fear you have been spending far too much time with the head gardener. Your good manners have suffered, and I might have to advise your mother to curtail your visits."

She sped ahead and breathlessly called back to him. "I was not alone with Gilchrist all morning, if *that* is what is vexing you."

Again, Darcy easily caught up with her. "Who else was there?"

She stopped to spare him an annoyed look. "Where, exactly, do you mean? In the woods? I saw a few squirrels scurrying about."

"Such insolence!" Darcy placed his large hands upon her thin upper arms. "Listen to me—"

Anne pulled away. "Leave me alone. I was in such good humour earlier, diverted beyond moderation. Now you are ruining it." Panting, she ran up the steps towards the garden entrance.

Darcy caught her by the sleeve, and a book dropped from under her arm. Leafing through it, he scoffed. "Is this your herbarium? It does not contain much. I had expected to see descriptions of plant specimens and, if apt, their healing properties."

Colour rose in Anne's cheeks as she snatched the Flora from him, clasping it against her breast. "Gilchrist and I have just begun." In a tone shifting from defensiveness to challenge, she added, "It is a respectable diversion. Botany is one of the few sciences considered appropriate for genteel women, and I shall not listen to any opposition."

"Just because you enjoy a diversion does not attest to its propriety. What occupied you and Gilchrist all that time? I witnessed you making sheep's eyes at him earlier."

Being two steps above, she stood nose-to-nose with him. "And I have witnessed the way *your* eyes fix upon Miss Bennet like a hungry little boy at Gunter's!" Turning and grabbing the latch, she flung open the door, barely missing Darcy's face with it.

He followed her into the library. "As difficult as it is for me to believe, I am beginning to entertain unsavoury suspicions about you and Gilchrist. For pity's sake, Anne, have a care for your reputation. Should my intuition prove unerring, shame will be brought to the noble name of your mother. Tell me now, are you engaged in some sort of a"—he swallowed hard—"liaison?"

"Lower your voice," she hissed, "lest servants as far as Rara Avis hear your salacious accusations." Under her breath, she muttered, "How did Miss Bennet put it? Ah yes. For a man of sense and education and who has lived in the world, you, Fitzwilliam Darcy, are a *nincompoop*! And furthermore, propriety and etiquette do not always equate with authentic goodness." She turned on her heel and fled the room.

Sinking into an upholstered armchair, Darcy leant forward, shoulders slumped. The cushions on the sofa across from him appeared faded, but his curiosity about such an anomaly was equally dull.

Head in hands, he thought his cousin was entirely correct in her estimation of him. *Nincompoop*. He had made so many mistakes—assuming Wickham was out of his life once and for all and hiring the nefarious Mrs Younge as Georgiana's companion. Those two errors in judgment had nearly led to his sister's ruination. Then he utterly had bungled his one and only attempt to woo a woman. And by giving Bingley disgraceful guidance, he had broken another lady's heart. Kind soul that Miss Elizabeth Bennet was, he had been forgiven for those trespasses—or so he hoped.

Have I now unfairly accused Anne of illicitness?

Heaving himself from the chair, Darcy decided another reckless ride might be in order, then he thought better of it. He would not put a horse in peril just because he, himself, had failed to put his best foot forward. Instead, he went for a brisk walk through the conifer plantation and contemplated his misdeeds.

Listening with half an ear to the rector's rambling sermon that Sunday, Darcy sat alongside his aunt in the righthand, frontmost pew—the one reserved for the de Bourgh family—and rested his eyes upon Elizabeth, across the aisle, next to Mrs Collins.

"Suffering," intoned the clergyman, "cannot conquer faith. Furthermore..."

Upon receiving a sudden pain in his right arm, Darcy glared at the offending bony elbow. Jabbed a second time, he assumed Lady Catherine had noticed his inattention. Bowing his head, he redirected his eyes to the floor. Her ladyship poked him a third time and asked for his pocket watch. Clearing her throat to capture the clergyman's attention, she held up the timepiece and tapped an impatient finger upon its face.

After that, the service concluded rather abruptly, and the relieved congregation filed out and stood about the churchyard, chatting.

Never a garrulous sort of person, Darcy made an effort to speak briefly to those with whom he was acquainted, all the while hoping for an opportunity to engage with a certain young lady from Hertfordshire and perhaps accompany her to the parsonage. On his way to her, he stopped and joined his cousin who was conversing with one of Rosings Park's leaseholders. The man recently had wed the daughter of another tenant, and the newly married couple stood side by side, sharing affectionate looks. His hand never left the small of her back, and she frequently smiled up at him.

Darcy longed for that same sort of attachment with Elizabeth, or rather, with her as Mrs Darcy.

Into the wee hours, he had lain awake, envisioning such a future. The yearning was a constant, physical ache, and he despaired of ever being able to change sufficiently to win her love.

Familiar, wholesome laughter rang out above all the hubbub and recollected Darcy to his surroundings. Turning, he espied Elizabeth smiling and chatting with the Collinses—*and Brinton, that popinjay, of all people!*

As parishioners dispersed, Darcy headed towards the Hunsford party, assuming they were taking leave of Mr Brinton.

Instead, upon witnessing Darcy's approach, the master of Rara Avis shepherded them into his carriage. "Sorry, old boy," he called out, "but I have room for only these three." Smiling his perfect smile, Mr Brinton gave him a jaunty salute and hopped aboard the vermilion landaulet.

The equipage carrying Lady Catherine, Anne, Mrs Jenkinson, and Dubois stopped alongside Darcy, but he shook his head at the coachman and said he would walk. Missing Fitzwilliam's companionship, he stopped at the stable to visit his own carriage horses. Refusing to feel sorry for himself, he admitted it was rather pitiful that he had sought the company of animals.

As the stable workers began returning from church, Darcy overheard their chatter, and it soon became evident they were unaware of his presence in the stall.

"There's a thief hereabouts. I heard so at Mrs Chapman's funeral, God rest her soul. Tommy, the errand boy, is Chapman's nephew, and he swears the de Bourgh gold and family silver—dishes, knives, and such—is being nicked."

"A younger voiced piped up. "The butler must have done it. He's the one responsible for the valuables, ain't he?"

"Aye," said one of the grooms, "but that ain't the only embarrassing fact the de Bourghs want kept secret. The frail young miss, who sat in church all innocent-like, goes to Gilchrist's cottage two or three times a week for hours at a time...but only weather permitting, mind."

As the group approached the nearby ladder, Darcy emerged from behind one of his matching bays and addressed the stable master. "Johnson, I should like a word with you."

That silenced the workers, who scrambled up the ladder to change out of their Sunday best before going about their duties. After giving the stable master a piece of his mind for allowing that sort of gossip from his underlings, Darcy walked out into the yard and chuckled at the erroneous gossip about plates being stolen.

When was the last time I laughed aloud? Days? A fortnight?

Feels like years. Even without someone to share in his mirth, it felt wonderful to laugh.

Sobering, he knew Elizabeth would take her leave of Kent the day following his cousin's celebratory ball. Therefore, he intended to properly woo the young lady, solve the thievery or vandalism, and discover what in the world his cousin had been up to during her outings.

And he had just over a se'nnight to accomplish all three tasks.

Somewhat of a snip, I should think.

Chapter Nine

Monday, April 13

Later than customary in the middle of the day, Elizabeth was in her room fastening her warm pelisse in preparation for a walk when a hurried and heavy tread pounded upon the stairs.

"Cousin Elizabeth! Cousin Elizabeth!" It was Mr Collins's frantic voice, portending either joyous tidings, doom and gloom, or new shelves in some closet. Opening her door in trepidation, she spotted him ascending, red-faced and gasping for breath.

"You will scarcely believe what has just occurred," he cried upon reaching the landing, advancing towards her, gesturing not unlike a windmill. "Come down. Come down at once! Make haste!"

Fetching her gloves and asking the nature of the emergency, Elizabeth could make no sense of his babble about her good fortune.

Quicker than was advisable for one so ungainly, her cousin clambered down the stairs until at the bottom he hustled Elizabeth out the front door. There, in the lane at the garden gate was Miss de Bourgh sitting in a park phaeton.

Bowing and scraping, Mr Collins rattled on about Miss de Bourgh's superlative presence and divine radiance gracing his humble premises. "And as you so graciously requested, here is my cousin."

The two young ladies greeted one another, and it was with great relief that Elizabeth discerned no physical harm had befallen Mr Darcy's cousin during Saturday's reckless drive. She suspected Miss de Bourgh's character was more complex and interesting than it appeared, for she had observed a perceptible sparkle, a telling gleam in her eye. And when the heiress thought no one was observing, a self-satisfied little smirk often played at the corners of her mouth. Such had been witnessed on those occasions when Lady Catherine had spoken of her daughter's poor health, the accomplishments she might have achieved if not for her frailty, and of her long-standing engagement to Mr Darcy.

The subject of her thoughts addressed her. "Although the sun deigns to shine, it has made little difference in the chill of the air. How providential to see you warmly dressed for an outing, for I have come with the express purpose of inviting you to join me on a jaunt. Will you accompany me?"

"Of course she will." Mr Collins clapped a palm to his black-clad breast. "You pay my poor cousin a great honour. Indeed, you do."

Elizabeth had anticipated a lovely walk alone with her thoughts, but she supposed an outing with the enigmatic heiress might prove enlightening. Shading her eyes against the sun, she accepted the invitation with thanks and added, "Never have I ridden in a phaeton before, but I have heard of their tipping over. I trust you do not drive with excessive speed."

"Cousin Elizabeth, you discredit Miss de Bourgh by implying such incautious behaviour. Never would the daughter of my patroness drive recklessly. As you see, her phaeton is not so very high—although as befitting her exalted station, it would be perfectly proper for her to sit far above others."

The little smirk played about Miss de Bourgh's lips. "The hour grows late. Your cousin and I must be on our way."

While he profusely apologised for keeping the heiress waiting in the cold, Mr Collins clumsily assisted Elizabeth in climbing aboard. Surrounded by upholstered squabs and with her lap covered by a heavy rug, she felt snug and secure as the pair of grey ponies surged forwards to trot along the lane.

Miss de Bourgh explained how the light-weight metals in her carriage's construction resulted in better suspension and ease of steering. "High phaetons do tend to tip over if one turns a corner too quickly, but I assure you that is not the case in a low one such as this."

Elizabeth held on as they navigated a sharp turn past Rosings Park's orangery. "Mr Darcy mentioned you are interested in botany and are compiling an herbarium. Will you be collecting specimens today?"

Gathering the reins in one hand, Miss de Bourgh patted the leather-bound book beside her on the seat. The word 'Flora' was embossed on its cover. "Patches of wood anemone were discovered in dappled shade near the deciduous copse, and my head gardener cut some for me. We are to fetch them now."

They stopped in front of a thatch-roofed cottage of Kentish ragstone. "This is, as Gilchrist calls it, his bothy." Book in hand, Miss de Bourgh hopped down and rapped at the door. "Gilchrist, are you there?" Receiving no response, she beckoned Elizabeth, then disappeared inside.

Feeling quite the trespasser, Elizabeth set foot in the tiny dwelling which was rich in specimens of nature. Mingled aromas of dried flowers hanging upside down from rafters and the herbs growing in windowsill pots evoked pleasant memories of Longbourn's fragrant still-room, striking her with a painful longing for her home, for her family.

"I was hoping you might meet Gilchrist today." Plucking anemones from a dish of water on the table, Miss de Bourgh carelessly tossed the wet flowers into her Flora.

When she noticed Elizabeth watching, she gave a little laugh. "I have only started my collection. So far, I have these anemones and a few wild cherry blossoms."

Elizabeth thought crumpled flowers pressed between two pages would look rather sad. Saying nothing, she glanced through illustrated editions of a botanical magazine and gardening manuals stacked upon the table. Her thoughts, however, turned to other words—ones written in a strong masculine hand in black ink upon hot-pressed letter paper of the finest quality. Lost in thought, she startled when Miss de Bourgh took her by the arm and moved towards the door.

"I am too eager and in too much of a hurry to wait for Gilchrist. I have a surprise for you, Miss Bennet."

There it was again—that telling gleam in her eye. Something was afoot, and Elizabeth did not care for surprises. As they took their places in the phaeton, she said, "Where is your Flora? Did you leave it behind?"

Urging her ponies to walk on, Miss de Bourgh gave an inelegant little shrug. "'Tis unimportant. I shall collect it another time."

Soon they passed wild cherry trees in bloom at the ancient woodland's edge. When they passed the place where she had encountered Mr Darcy, Elizabeth insisted upon knowing their destination.

Aiming her whip southwards, Miss de Bourgh grinned. "We are for Rara Avis, the small estate bordering Rosings."

Such information provided no comfortable feeling.

"Rara Avis? But that is where Mr Brinton resides, is it not?" Miss de Bourgh nodded in acknowledgement, and Elizabeth's concern grew apace. "Is it not rather late in the day for making calls? And is there a *Mrs* Brinton to receive us?"

At a crack of the whip, the phaeton gained speed. "No. He is a bachelor."

Gaping at the young lady, Elizabeth cried, "Then we cannot possibly go there alone!"

"We are not alone. We have each other." Growing more animated, Miss de Bourgh spoke in fulsome praise of Rara Avis, its manor, grounds, plants, and birds. "You will be delighted with the place, I promise. I saw you chatting and laughing with Mr Brinton after church yesterday. Did you not think him charming? The good humour of his countenance is bewitching, is it not?" Without awaiting an answer, she nudged Elizabeth and gave her a wink. "Laurence Brinton is not only single. He is singular!"

Botheration. "Please tell me you are not playing at matchmaking and *that* is not the reason for our journey thither."

"No, no, not at all, although I do hope to cultivate an intimate acquaintance between you and Mr Brinton." The phaeton was masterfully steered round a sharp bend. "I should warn you, however, that the gentleman is considered the black sheep of his family, and his notions of decorum are not as strict as, say, Darcy's. And speaking of that cousin of mine"—Miss de Bourgh made a face—"what is your opinion of *him*? Have you, like certain ladies of the *ton*, set your cap at Fitzwilliam Darcy? Do you lie awake at night and think of him with excessive awe and infatuation?"

Elizabeth scoffed. "Most certainly not." *I shall not denigrate the gentleman, but I will be honest.* "He did not make a favourable first impression in my neighbourhood, but he improves upon further acquaintance. The more I come to know him, the more sensibly I understand his disposition. As for infatuation, no. He is far too taciturn and arrogant for my liking. We are complete opposites."

After reading his letter, though, Elizabeth had been well pleased with the conversations they had, and if she were honest with herself, she had not entirely loathed sparring with him months ago at Netherfield.

Miss de Bourgh gave a merry little laugh, a sound previously unheard from her. "Arrogant, oh yes. But taciturn? Rarely do I have an opportunity to observe him in social settings amongst strangers, but with family and intimate friends, he can be talkative enough. In fact—at least with me—he can be rather *too* fond of expressing himself, making speeches, giving lectures, and issuing orders."

Elizabeth could well imagine that.

Passing through an expanse of conifers and hoping to dispel a degree of anxiety, she inhaled deeply, closing her eyes, sensing the humus below and the refreshing, resinous scents of the surrounding pine, spruce, and fir trees. No insects buzzed, no birds sang, no squirrels scuttled. The silence of the woodland was disturbed only by her thoughts and Miss de Bourgh's resumption.

"Despite my complaints, I am inordinately fond of Darcy. He possesses those virtues expected of a *true* gentleman, such as courtesy, refinement, honesty, and generosity." Elizabeth gave an incredulous, scornful little laugh. "You scoff again, Miss Bennet, but you must understand he is amongst the one or two hundred wealthiest men in England. To be distinguished by the master of Pemberley is something, indeed. Ergo, he is very careful about paying particular attention to any woman or asking them to stand up with him. Dancing with Darcy, you see, confers a special importance upon a lady. You may wonder why I shall not marry him, but all I shall say for now is that I have no desire to be mistress of Pemberley. I have other plans."

Interesting, but what would she say if she learnt he had distinguished me and conferred upon me a most significant importance? Still, Elizabeth's judgment could not be impartial concerning his merit. "Your cousin does not even *like* to dance, particularly with young ladies who have been slighted by other men or with those who are only tolerable and not handsome enough to tempt him."

"You sound embittered." Reining in her ponies beneath a budding deciduous canopy, Miss de Bourgh studied Elizabeth. "Did Darcy speak so disrespectfully to you?"

Bowing her head, Elizabeth fidgeted with the rug's fringe. "Not directly, but he must have known I could hear him. To have spoken so insultingly demonstrated complete indifference to my sensibilities as well as my reputation in my neighbourhood."

She rubbed her brow. *I thought I had forgiven him for that. Why must I dwell upon it?* "I beg your pardon. Your cousin did apologise for those remarks, and I should not have made mention of them."

"Do not fret. One of these fine days, Darcy will have his comeuppance. Some clever, spirited woman will put him in his place. I have endeavoured to do so, but such an inflated opinion of one's eminence is not easily damped, is it?"

Set into motion again, the phaeton soon turned away from the wooded track, onto the road, down a tree-lined lane, and up to the manor's gravel sweep at Rara Avis.

Chapter Ten

Rara Avis was a pretty prospect, but Anne could tell Miss Bennet thought it unworthy of extravagant praise.

A groom arrived to take charge of the equipage, and as the ladies stood at the bottom of the steps, Brinton rushed down them.

His white shirt was marred by dried dabs of yellow and blue paint in a larger splotch of scarlet. Black breeches, stockings, house slippers, and an unbuttoned, striped vermilion and chartreuse waistcoat completed his eccentric appearance. *Good grief! With that tousled hair and those rolled up shirtsleeves, he looks like an unkempt beggar.*

Arms stretched wide, Brinton approached. "Anne! How exceedingly good it is to see you."

Not bothering to conceal her astonishment at his *déshabillé,* Miss Bennet whispered to Anne, "Obviously, we were not expected."

"And Miss Elizabeth Bennet! I am overjoyed to welcome you to my home." Reaching for her hand, the master of Rara Avis bowed over it. An ebony curl, longer than fashionable, fell over one of his eyes. Graceful, paint-stained fingers brushed it back into some semblance of order before he placed Miss Bennet's hand upon his forearm and covered it with his own. She flinched, and Anne supposed the lady never before, even with gloved fingers, had touched a man's exposed skin.

"Do come in, ladies, and view my latest creation. Then we shall nibble on currant cakes, drink tea, chat, and have a pleasant afternoon. And," he said, smiling at Anne, "because I dearly love to dance, I now request, in advance, a set with each of you at my dear friend's ball."

Anne could tell Miss Bennet was taken aback by the gentleman's familiar manner. *But I am certain there is so much kindliness in his reception she cannot help but be charmed.*

Miss Bennet murmured, "We should *not* be here."

In less than ten minutes, as Anne expected, Brinton—being his customary, likeable self—had enchanted Miss Bennet.

I daresay she cannot help but succumb to his allure. But perhaps it is the other way round, judging by the way he has yet to remove his hand from where it rests upon hers. How terribly interesting. Yes, terribly so.

Having been energetic in promoting Rara Avis and its dashing owner during the drive thither, Anne suspected her efforts might have been, to some degree, overly zealous. A feeling, almost akin to envy, arose within her breast.

Balderdash! Although the society of so talented, so clever, and so jovial a gentleman gradually had become Anne's most exquisite pleasure, it was not as though she were in love with Brinton. She was certainly *not* jealous.

Trailing behind, she observed them, talking and laughing, winding through long passages and up several staircases. Every moment there, every turn about the place, seemed to supply Miss Bennet with a new delight. Anne remembered feeling that same sort of awe during her own early visits. The manor brimmed with exotic potted plants, songbirds in ornate cages, stained glass windows, Brinton's works of art, musical instruments, and curiosities from round the world.

"Just one more flight," Brinton said, "then we shall reach my garret."

Miss Bennet bestowed her delightful smile upon him. "Garret, sir? You paint a dismal image—a cold, wretched abode for an artist."

Earlier, she had complimented a few of his landscapes on display, but Miss Bennet had yet to hear him recite his verses or perform sweet, haunting, intricate melodies on the violin. It seemed to Anne that Laurence Brinton was the living embodiment of the extraordinary men of centuries past who had created masterpieces during the revival of learning. She, however, may have been biased.

"Here we are." He opened the door. Sunlight flooded

the sky parlour, streaming through windows on three sides and in the roof.

Anne had been there only twice before. There were too many stairs for her liking, and she was panting, while Miss Bennet was scarcely out of breath. *It must be all those walks she is so fond of taking.*

The garret was warm, and sweat beaded on Anne's forehead until her mother's voice reminded her that ladies did not sweat; they perspired. As delicately as possible, she mopped her brow with a handkerchief.

Miss Bennet cried in delight upon seeing the pair of colourful popinjays upon their perch.

"Ah yes. Meet Squeak and Squawk." Brinton grimaced. "They were named by sailors who abducted them from *La Isla de la Trinidad*. Their previous owner—from whom I rescued them—kept those horrid names, and my lovelies were so accustomed to Squeak and Squawk that I had not the heart to change them."

He spoke to the parrots, and one of them made a loud, harsh reply of sorts. "During warm weather, these beauties reside in the aviary, but it is presently far too cold for my pets out there in the garden. What a beastly, cold spring we are having." Holding out his hand, he made kissing noises. One of the macaws—Anne did not know which—flapped its wings and flew over, landing on his wrist. Miss Bennet gently stroked the macaw's scarlet head while Brinton fed it some sort of nut.

Anne wrinkled her nose. *He is talking to the bird in the same sickening manner Mrs Jenkinson uses when cooing at infants.*

Ugh. I could never utter such meaningless twaddle. Besides, I do not want children.

After setting the bird upon its perch, Brinton theatrically unveiled the oil painting he wanted the ladies to see. Anne's gasp was echoed by Miss Bennet's.

"That is *me*," Anne cried, aghast, "holding Squeak...or Squawk. Heaven and earth, Brinton! What am I *wearing*?" Ready to swoon, Anne fetched the sterling silver vinaigrette from her reticule, opened the lid, and deeply inhaled its pungent infusion of ammonia, vinegar, alcohol, and lemon oil. Her nose ran. Her eyes stung. Her sensibilities were aggrieved.

Sounding utterly bewildered, Brinton asked, "Anne, have I offended you?"

Good grief. The loveable muttonhead lives life without fear and without regard for others' judgments or criticisms. Anne knew that surrendering to society's expectations would prove downright dull, if not malignant, to Brinton.

"How could you portray me like that?" She glared at the portrait, then at him. "When did you paint that travesty?"

"I frequently make sketches of your face, Anne, you know that. I have shown them to you." Appearing somewhat dejected, he gripped a fistful of the shirt covering his chest. "Admittedly, I took certain liberties in depicting your form and mode of dress, but—"

"Mode of dress? That gown is practically indecent!" Anne squeezed her eyes shut. "Paint over it, Brinton. Paint me a dark-hued velvet gown with some sleeves and a high neck."

Turning, she glared at Miss Bennet, for she had just heard a barely suppressed laugh. *Her blushing face is a mask of gravity, but those expressive eyes betray her mirth.*

Anne stamped her foot. "This is *not* amusing!"

"Tut, tut." Brinton patted Anne's shoulder, then turned to throw a sheet over the easel. "Such a pity. You often lament the dowdy fashions your mother insists you wear, so I thought you would be pleased with that portrait."

Anne knew how much he loved sharing his talents and happiness with others, and she regretted her angry outburst. "I promise I shall be pleased with it once you properly clothe me."

From the parrots' perch came squawks that sounded suspiciously like, "Heaven and earth, Brinton! What am I *wearing*? Heaven and earth, Brinton! What am I *wearing*?"

It was all too much. Anne had had enough. Enervated, she trudged over to the garret's sofa and collapsed amongst its colourful silk cushions. *Hang this frailty of mine!*

Thankfully, the outlandish clock on the cabinet informed her they had overstayed their welcome. *Well, not really. I know Brinton would like us to remain, but the man has no sense of time. I doubt he even owns a pocket watch. He lives in, and strictly for, the moment.*

But she could not risk her mother's wrath or, *heaven forfend,* Darcy's. And Mrs Collins would fret should her houseguest not arrive at the parsonage in a timely manner. Anne did not even want to think about the panic Mr

Collins would be in should the daughter of his patroness be assumed missing.

"We must leave." Grabbing her reticule and stumbling down the staircases, Anne called for her pelisse and phaeton. Miss Bennet and Brinton slowly followed in her footsteps.

Calmer then, Anne reflected on their visit. If one blotted out the memory of a certain scandalous oil painting, she believed the brief call had served its purpose. Like Gilchrist, Brinton was a willing partner in their scheme. And never would she unscrupulously control or influence a friend.

Anne was growing rather fond of Elizabeth Bennet, and she hoped her new friend would not regret her involvement, albeit in a secondary role. *She must not become truly enamoured of Brinton, for I would not like to be responsible for another person's heartbreak. I have anxious considerations enough as it is.*

In a rush to return to Rosings, Anne had left her gloves at Rara Avis, and Miss Bennet insisted they take turns wearing hers. The shy sun had hidden itself behind clouds, and Anne, chilled to the marrow and craving her fireside and a bit of Mrs Jenkinson's incessant coddling, urged her ponies from a slow jog into a lively trot.

Stifling a sigh, she answered another of Miss Bennet's endless enquiries about Brinton. "He recently turned six and twenty, and before you ask, yes, he has an inheritance from his parents. After their deaths, he was raised by a wealthy great-uncle, the owner of Brinton Hall. When that gentleman died, my friend inherited his ancestral home and re-named it Rara Avis, which means rare bird. And he *is* a rare bird, indeed. Amiable, he is liked by almost everyone save my mother and Darcy who think he is an immature, selfish, and irresponsible young man who flits from one interest to another."

"Does he flit from one *woman* to another?"

Passing out of the woods into the park, Anne watched a robin tilt its head, listening for a worm in the thawing ground. Mimicking its sideways movement, she contrived an answer. "No doubt you have discerned that Brinton is an audacious flirt. Thus far he has shied away from marriage."

Best change that *subject!* "He has many friends, ones who understand him. He mingles with politicians and artists alike, including Byron. He does not, however, tolerate people who belittle him. He likes happy people and—"

A rider approached at a gallop, and Anne pulled back on the reins. "Oh good grief! Is that *Darcy*?"

For the better part of an hour, Darcy had been sequestered with the butler and housekeeper as they tried in vain to get to the bottom of the recent mischief. According to Mr Harris and Mrs White, the whereabouts of all maids and footmen had been accounted for each time damage had occurred, including the previous night during which time the manor's doors and windows had been tightly locked.

The only members of the household not already questioned about the thievery or vandalism were Dubois and Mrs Jenkinson, and both were above reproach. Darcy acknowledged such interviews had to be undertaken but was reluctant to interrogate two ladies of genteel birth.

Before speaking to his cousin's abigail and elderly companion, he had hoped to call on Elizabeth and partake of her delightful society. Lost in pleasurable thoughts as he descended the stairs, he hummed a tune, then nearly jumped out of his skin when from below his aunt's voice boomed like thunder.

"Darcy! Have you seen your intended today?"

"Thus far, I have not had that pleasure." *But I am on my way to the parsonage, where I shall properly woo the woman intended for me.*

Impatient at being waylaid, he checked his pocket watch and spoke in haste. "I assume you erroneously refer to Anne as my intended."

"Of course I do!" One of Lady Catherine's bejewelled hands splayed across her neck. "What do you mean *erroneously*? Stars and garters! Who else could possibly be your intended?"

"I must remind you, my lady, that your daughter and I are not engaged, and in so speaking, you run the risk of damaging her reputation." Darcy had spoken with unwavering firmness, but as ever, his reminder was ignored.

Studying his person with evident suspicion, Lady Catherine eventually gave him a rare smile, and a speculative gleam shone in her eyes. "You look particularly dapper this morning. Having applied yourself so well to your appearance, I trust you will be requesting a private audience with Anne as soon as she is returned." Though muttered, her next remark was audible. "That girl needs a husband."

In point of fact, Darcy had gone back to his chambers following the meeting with the two senior servants. His hair had required a good combing after being tousled and tangled in frustration over the devilry being perpetrated.

Jonesby, his valet, had helped him don a flattering bottle-green coat and handed him a comfit of anise, caraway, and fennel seeds to freshen his breath after too much coffee. That second toilette of the morning was not, however, for Anne's benefit.

Knowing her ladyship's temper never could bear opposition well, Darcy was disinclined to make complicated matters more awkward. Choosing to save himself from useless remonstrance, he simply avoided the subject. "I was considering speaking with Mrs Jenkinson and Dubois regarding the vandalism. Have you asked them, or the stable workers, about Anne's current whereabouts, or shall I?"

"It goes without saying that I have done so. I am exceedingly attentive to such things, you know. Dubois said she helped Anne into her riding habit, and John Coachman reported that my daughter went out in her phaeton over an hour ago. No one has seen her since. This is a most vexing concern. Until recently, it has not been like Anne to disappear without letting us know her plans." Turning on her heel, Lady Catherine walked towards the library. "Favour me with your company. I must speak to you in private."

With a longing look towards the front door, Darcy followed.

As soon as the library door closed behind them, his aunt took the most comfortable chair for herself and indicated where he should sit. Rearranging her shawl, she began in anger. "Prevailing reports of a most alarming nature reached me hours ago when my coachman told me of Anne's frequent and protracted visits to Gilchrist's cottage. I could not like his implication of unseemly goings-on."

"Did he say as much?"

"Of course not, and he should mind his tongue if he values his position. A tryst! Can you imagine the scandal? The disparity of an earl's niece and a gardener!" Fanning her flushed face, she gave a dismissive, unladylike snort. "This is all because of that botany hobby of hers. Now, you see how greatly your dear cousin has been traduced. Though I know it can be naught but a scandalous invention, such ignoble slander cannot and will not be tolerated. I insist upon having these disgraceful reports universally contradicted. *You* hired Gilchrist, and *you* must see to the matter at once."

Although not entirely free of apprehension in that same regard, Darcy remained silent about his suspicions. A sense of duty to his relations ever ready, he reluctantly postponed calling at the parsonage and promised his aunt he would speak to the gardener.

The gleam was back in her ladyship's eyes. "Very good. I shall anticipate a favourable report from you later and a joyful announcement from you and Anne this evening."

* * *

On his way to Gilchrist's cottage to confront him about his possible involvement with Anne, Darcy fervently prayed he would not discover the two of them in any sort of compromising position.

Upon finding the cottage unoccupied, he glanced about. *What is this doing here?* With a huff of disgust, he picked up Anne's Flora and tucked it under an arm.

After wandering about the grounds, he espied Gilchrist in one of the greenhouses.

The air was hot as he stepped inside, yet there was a chill in Darcy's reception as he asked whether the master gardener knew Anne's whereabouts. Gilchrist said he had not seen her that morning.

"Then, how do you account for this?" From behind his back, Darcy produced his cousin's Flora and slammed it on a nearby potting table. "I found it in your cottage." Jaw jutting, he ground out, "On your rumpled cot."

Seemingly unconcerned, the gardener shrugged. "She must have stopped by the bothy while I was out. The anemones I saved for her are gone."

Nearly matched in height, the two men stood toe to toe. Damping down anger, Darcy spoke in an even tone. "Do you have any notion where she might be now?"

Without answering for himself, Gilchrist beckoned one of the nearby underlings and asked if he had seen Miss de Bourgh that day.

"Aye," a young lad replied. "I saw her with a pretty young lady driving into the woods about an hour ago."

Darcy ordered everyone, save the master gardener, from the hothouse. "Look me in the eye, Gilchrist, and tell me you have not laid a hand upon my cousin."

There was a tightness in the Scot's eyes as he turned and swore he had not. His unflinching gaze bore into Darcy's as he admitted to a platonic friendship with Miss de Bourgh, nothing more.

Added to that, Gilchrist's insistence that he was far too busy with spring planting in the formal, kitchen, herb, and scent gardens to spend much time assisting Anne with the herbarium also bore truth. Therefore, Darcy was inclined to believe him. But there followed such an angry spate of Scottish burr that he had difficulty following it, and the man's gruffness made reserve impossible.

Neck and jaw rigid, Darcy drew himself up taller. "Lady Catherine will be informed of the insolent manner in which you—"

The gardener said such a complaint would be of little concern, and he gladly would return to his former employer. Mr Brinton, he said, had complete faith in his abilities while Darcy's termagant of an aunt mistrusted his horticultural knowledge.

Good character was paramount in a gardener. *What had I been thinking to have hired such a surly fellow? Another of my mistakes.* Stepping closer and having a fraction of an inch height on the inflexible Scot, Darcy calmly said, "In that case, Gilchrist, you may leave at once. You are hereby dismissed from employment at Rosings."

Gilchrist turned away to fuss with one of the new varieties of rose he was cultivating.

Momentarily distracted by the blush-hued bloom, Darcy pictured Elizabeth's lips and imagined their softness and warmth. Stepping forwards, he plucked one of the petals and placed it in his breast pocket.

* * *

Outside the stable, his agitation beyond expression, Darcy tucked Anne's Flora in his saddlebag. Riding out of the park and onto the lane in search of his cousin, he prayed she had not gone astray, in any manner.

Just as his horse had been urged into a gallop, a light carriage pulled by two grey ponies approached at a lively trot. *Anne!* Darcy hauled back on the reins while she did the same to hers.

Feelings in sudden warfare, he was delighted upon recognising the passenger, relieved his cousin was safe, but still angry about Gilchrist. Stopping abreast of the phaeton, he tipped his hat and forced a smile.

"Good day, Miss Bennet." In a less pleasant tone, he asked his cousin where she had been.

"Good day to you, too, Darcy." Anne gave him a wide-eyed, innocent look. "As you see, I have taken Miss Bennet for a nice little jaunt."

"You have been gone for well over an hour." Darcy lowered his head, glaring at her from under his hat's brim. "Your mother is concerned. Where, exactly, were you all that time?"

"We stopped by Gilchrist's cottage to fetch the anemones he picked for my Flora."

"Yes, yes, I know that. But where did you go afterwards?"

"We drove through the plantation." His cousin gave him a sugar-sweet smile. "Now we are on the lane, heading back to the parsonage."

Not unlike the three horses, Darcy breathed noisily through his nose. "It does *not* take an hour to drive through the woods."

Eyes softening, voice gentling, he leant forwards. "Miss Bennet, would *you* be so kind as to tell me where you were between the woods and here? And please do not say Rara Avis." Her rosebud blush matched her tempting lips, and Darcy's heart throbbed against the petal in his breast pocket.

Elizabeth glanced at Anne, then looked straight at him. "Very well, sir, I shall not."

Darcy's eyes flew wide, and he detected a fleeting quirk of her lips. *Saucy little minx!*

"Do not be so dull and unadventurous, Darcy," said Anne. "Yes, we went there. I wanted my dear new friend to see the place."

A feeling of dread overcame him, and Darcy's hands clenched on the reins. "From afar, I trust."

In a most unladylike manner, Anne rolled her eyes. "Even had *I* foolishly planned on us—two single, ingenuous ladies—calling on a bachelor, do you suppose Miss Bennet here would have consented to such scandalous behaviour?" She looked as though butter would not melt in her mouth.

His heart's desire's expression, however, indicated she obviously wished herself elsewhere, somewhere far, far removed from the cousins.

To regard Elizabeth Bennet with anything less than esteem was utterly unthinkable. Darcy tore his eyes away from that lady's lovely countenance and caught the smug smile on his cousin's face. *Cunning little brat!*

With a saucy grin, a forceful shake of the reins, and a mighty 'Gee!', Anne urged her ponies to race away from him.

He might have been mistaken, but when he thought about it, Darcy could have sworn his cousin was wearing gloves that were too big for her and that Elizabeth's hands were bare.

With cold fingers, Elizabeth held fast to her bonnet as the phaeton lurched ahead and raced along the lane. Above the clatter of ponies' hooves, she heard Mr Darcy's shout as his horse gave chase.

Miss de Bourgh's voice rose above the carriage's rattles and the rushing wind. "Can you keep a secret?"

Elizabeth did not want to become embroiled in any further subterfuge. "Yes, I *can*. But I choose not to hear whatever you wish to divulge. Please do not involve me in your intrigues."

When the heiress took her eyes off the road and glanced at her, Elizabeth wondered whether the remorseful look spoke of guilt or of regret.

Eyes fixed straight ahead then, Miss de Bourgh masterfully steered her ponies past the parsonage and towards Rosings.

"You are coming home with me. With you by my side, neither Mother nor Darcy will dare chastise me. Besides, I wish to show you the glorious gown I shall wear to the ball." Reaching over, she covered Elizabeth's bare hand with her gloved one and beseeched, "Stay with me. Please."

Botheration! On second thought, she realised Mrs Collins would be at Mr Chapman's with her basketful of foodstuffs, and Elizabeth wanted to avoid being alone with Mr Collins and his prattle. It was a draw, but as long as Miss de Bourgh did not solicit her involvement in any sort of collusion, Elizabeth would rather spend time with Mr Darcy's cousin than with her own.

"Why yes, I shall be delighted."

When Elizabeth walked into the parlour arm-in-arm with Miss de Bourgh, Lady Catherine's air was even more than customarily ungracious. Her ladyship's beady eyes burnt as brightly and looked twice as hard as the gemstones flashing upon her fingers.

Deigning to grace Elizabeth with a slight inclination of her head, Lady Catherine spoke with stiff politeness. "Miss Bennet, I was not expecting you."

"She is *my* guest, Mother." Miss de Bourgh offered Elizabeth an apology, a seat, and refreshments. The first two were accepted, the latter politely declined.

Lady Catherine spoke in hushed tones. "Where have you been, Anne?"

The heavy tread of boots, echoing from the great hall and drawing near the parlour, belonged to Mr Darcy, who then appeared in the doorway.

"Ladies." He bowed but said he could not join them. "I have urgent business to which I must attend. Just in time for spring planting, I am afraid I have summarily dismissed Gilchrist from employment here at Rosings and must find a replacement. I shall explain later." He bowed again. "Miss Bennet." With that, he turned away.

Miss de Bourgh jumped to her feet, and her pinched face turned an alarming shade of red. Then she dashed to the door in a flurry of voluminous riding-habit skirts. "Darcy, stop right there! What did you say to Gilchrist? I hope you did not offend him. He does not appreciate anyone questioning either his knowledge or his integrity. Besides, you cannot send Gilchrist away. He is *my* employee, and I shall not have it! Do you hear me?"

Certain she had heard the gentleman reply 'No' before the bickering cousins moved down the hall, Elizabeth—barely stifling a giggle—bowed her head and bit her lip. Once she had herself under control, she said, "My apologies, Lady Catherine, but with your permission, I should return to the parsonage now."

The instant Elizabeth stood to make an eager escape, Lady Catherine raised her voice. "Not so hasty, if you please. Where did you and Anne go today? I warn you, I am not to be trifled with. Though I had not thought you lost to every feeling of propriety and delicacy, I suspect you somehow have led my daughter astray. If Sir Lewis were still alive, he would be turning over in his grave!"

At Elizabeth's grin, Lady Catherine's eyes narrowed into slits. "I fail to find humour in this, young lady! Now, I insist upon knowing the truth. Were the two of you at Gilchrist's cottage? Did you leave Anne alone there with that man?"

Perhaps at her ladyship's age—no doubt similar to Mama's—one tends towards captiousness. Both of them certainly have no difficulty finding fault with me. "We paid a call there to collect anemones, but the gardener was not at home."

Breathless, Miss de Bourgh rushed back into the room. "Miss Bennet, I beg your pardon for abandoning you. Oh! Surely, you are not leaving, are you?"

Elizabeth nodded. "I feel I must."

"No. No, you cannot go without seeing my gown." Miss de Bourgh tugged Elizabeth's arm. "Come up to my apartments, please."

Thinking her rather pitiable, Elizabeth had not the heart to deny the entreaty. *She seems so desperate for a friend.*

As the two young ladies ascended the grand staircase, Miss de Bourgh had yet to let go of Elizabeth's arm. "Would you henceforth call me Anne?"

"If you wish. But, in turn, you must call me Elizabeth." She could not lament the acquaintance. Surely, it was not pity she felt but something more meaningful—the burgeoning of true friendship. In addition to being of an age, they shared something else in common. *Ignominious mothers.*

"Miss de Bourgh, *Anne,* speaking of gowns, I had no notion of attending a ball when my trunks were packed. However, I did bring one I wore last November at a private ball at which Mr Darcy and I stood up together for a set. So he has seen—"

Stepping away, Anne turned to face her. "I distinctly remember your telling me he did *not* dance with you because you were not handsome enough to tempt him. Good heavens, my friend! If that cousin of mine danced with you, conferring that special importance I mentioned, that means he *likes* you!"

Taking her by the arm again, she tut-tutted. "Do not fret. My lady's maid, Dubois, is adept with needle and thread. I shall have her embellish your gown in such a way that Darcy will not recognise it." Elizabeth demurred, but her protests fell upon deaf ears.

As they moved through the manor's maze of wings, galleries, and long passages with rooms opening off them, Elizabeth became entirely disoriented. *If ever left to find my way out of this place, I might never escape. They will find my desiccated skeleton in some closet or other. With shelves, no doubt.*

Eventually shown through Anne's apartments, Elizabeth thought them everything that money and good taste could provide.

Seated then in the commodious dressing room, the luxury of her surroundings faded to inconsequence when Anne proudly held up a sleek gown of ivory taffeta.

"Imagine, if you will, Elizabeth, this garment devoid of all its beautiful embroidery. *That* would be the gown my mother, even now, expects me to wear to the ball. But clever Dubois here"—she indicated the maid standing in the shadows—"spent endless hours sewing these narrow, indigo stripes and this spiralling, floral pattern upon it."

With a deep-blue fabric draped over one arm, the lady's maid stepped into the light. "Ah, but my masterpiece is this addition which I have yet to finish embellishing," she said in a faint French accent.

Anne took the darker garment and wrapped it round the gown, fastening it beneath the bodice. "Voilà! It is now an open robe. And do you see how Dubois has copied the gown's design onto the robe but in golden threads? It will shimmer in candlelight." She swayed the gown back and forth, making the robe billow. "But what is truly exciting is that, behind closed doors, I have been embroidering—"

Dubois cleared her throat. "Mademoiselle?"

"Oh Dubois! Surely we can let Elizabeth know of our—"

From somewhere in the apartments, Lady Catherine's voice calling for her daughter sent employer and maid into a flurry of activity, and they disappeared with the gown to secret it away.

While Elizabeth waited for Anne's return, Lady Catherine entered the dressing room. "Miss Bennet! *Now* what have you done with my daughter?"

Chapter Thirteen

Tuesday, April 14

Frequent downpours intermixed with sleet prevented Darcy from walking to the parsonage. Putting servants to the bother of preparing his carriage in a deluge for such a short distance was unthinkable. *As unthinkable as calling on Elizabeth Bennet while looking like a drowned rat and feeling not much better.* Consequently, he cursed the foul weather that suspended his wooing of the young lady and left him in the company of his aunt, his cousin, and the drowsy Mrs Jenkinson.

In disgrace due to her suspicious outings to Gilchrist's cottage, his cousin sat in sullen unresponsiveness while Lady Catherine gave way to violent indignation.

"Think, Anne! You are an heiress, the wealthy daughter of the late Sir Lewis de Bourgh, a niece of the current Earl of Matlock, and granddaughter of his predecessor. A woman of the upper classes does *not* cavort with a gardener! Your conduct has become most vexatiously provoking, and you are forbidden from visiting that man ever again."

Darcy agreed with his aunt. Why, such a class difference would make an alliance between Elizabeth and himself seem almost like one of equality! The thought gave him pause. *Apparently, one's opinion of one's own consequence is not easily damped.*

To escape the womenfolk, he went to the billiards room and played alone, cursing Colonel Fitzwilliam's superiors for calling him away. Then he sequestered himself in the library with the groundsman who, until a replacement for Gilchrist could be hired, agreed to temporarily add the head gardener's duties to his own responsibilities.

Wednesday, April 15

Darcy met with the estate manager to ensure the farms were well run and the tenant cottages in good repair. They discussed the problem of the late planting and adjusted their plans for a profitable autumn harvest. When the man left, Darcy turned towards the window to ruminate and glare at the accursed raindrops running down the pane. The curtains captured his attention, and he would have sworn they used to have a pattern stitched upon them. He sprang from the chair. *Blast!* It was past time to interrogate Mrs Jenkinson and Dubois.

After he had requested her presence in the library and asked a few leading questions, Anne's elderly companion shook her head and expressed concern about the goings-on.

"So very peculiar, is it not? And so suspect, too. Now, Mr Darcy, if you will excuse me, I must ensure your cousin's comfort." Shuffling her way to the door, she grumbled about the weather.

Darcy sighed. He had gleaned nothing, other than the fact that coldness and dampness had an adverse effect on the woman's rheumatism.

The abigail's interview proved to be another awkward affair. The refined lady was not only a French émigré but some sort of relation of Darcy's late uncle, Sir Lewis.

"I cannot help you, Mr Darcy," she said in her appealing accent, adding a Gallic shrug for good measure. Dubois then reminded him that she reported and answered directly to Anne, but she agreed the disappearances were a matter of great interest to her. *"Comme c'est très mystérieux!"*

Darcy had known questioning two such genteel ladies would be pointless.

Thursday, April 16

A variety of sporadic precipitation continued to fall, but Darcy craved escape. His spirits were jaded from writing odious business letters, rereading books, playing cards with the ladies, and listening to all the nonsense being uttered by them. He longed for playful impertinence, and as he explained to his aunt, he felt an overwhelming desire to call on the Collinses.

"How can you be so asinine as to think of such a thing, Darcy? I shall not hear of it. You must stay here and entertain Anne."

His cousin leant forwards in her chair. "If you do go, would you be so kind as to fetch a package for me? Miss Bennet should have something for Dubois."

Darcy agreed with alacrity while gaining his feet.

"Sit down!" Her ladyship gave a dissatisfied sniff when he did not comply. "The weather is ghastly. You will not be fit to be seen when you get there."

"A gentleman cannot always be within doors. I have grown restless. The parsonage is not far."

"I do not understand this sudden urge to call upon *those* people in this weather when you could stay here, warm and dry, and in more exalted and cherished company." With a twitch of her head, indicating her daughter, Lady Catherine gave Darcy a significant look that signified nothing at all to him. At his blank expression, she heaved a sigh. "Oh very well. At least, take a footman with an umbrella. If nothing else, *he* may have some sense."

Excusing himself, Darcy bounded up the stairs, and upon reaching his apartments, removed his coat. "Jonesby, I wish to exchange this waistcoat for the one that, according to you, matches my eyes...not that I am such a dandy to care about such things. Quickly, man."

Darcy shrugged off the buff-coloured waistcoat and waited and waited. "Jonesby, what the blazes is taking so long?"

The embarrassed valet returned from the dressing room empty-handed, save for a gold coin he handed to his master. "My apologies, sir. The indigo waistcoat appears to be missing. I distinctly remember unpacking it and storing it in the clothes press. However, when I looked in the appropriate drawer, all I found was that guinea."

Darcy heaved a heavy sigh. The theft was different from all the other disappearances, and someone clearly had no notion of the cost of a simple waistcoat. *A guinea! To quote Dubois, how very mysterious.*

"And have you read that one, Miss Bennet?" In the parlour at Hunsford, Darcy pointed to a table upon which rested a copy of *Gulliver's Travels*.

"Go on, Eliza." Mrs Collins smiled. "I know you are itching to say it."

Elizabeth's eyes lit with mirth. "I did, indeed, read *Gulliver's Travels*, sir. Rather *swiftly*, in fact."

Darcy did not care for wordplay in any form, and he was the wretchedest being in the world when it came to courteous falsehoods, but for her benefit alone, he smiled.

"Speaking of travellers' tales, did you know that Mr Brinton keeps journals of his many journeys abroad?"

He knew she and his cousin had been at Rara Avis. But for what duration were they there? Had Elizabeth enjoyed the man's company? "I suppose he regaled you with colourful accounts of his visits to faraway lands."

Tilting her head, Elizabeth gave him a puzzled look. "No, he made no mention of such. I viewed a few of his paintings and met a pair of macaws. Oh, and Mr Brinton requested sets with your cousin and me at her ball."

Darcy damped down the tinge of jealousy heating his blood. "Then may *I* have the honour of standing up with you for *two* sets, one preferably being the supper?"

He heard a little gasp from Mrs Collins, and upon granting him the requested set and another of his choice, a pretty blush overspread Elizabeth's cheeks.

Dare I request the first or last? Then he remembered promising to dance the opening set with his cousin. *Blast!* He leant in. "Would you grant me the great honour of your last?"

Still blushing, Elizabeth nodded.

"Well, now that *that* is settled," said Mrs Collins, drawing Darcy's attention away from her captivating friend, "shall I fetch my husband from writing Sunday's sermon and set up a table for whist?"

"A moment please, if you will." Darcy smiled at the lady of the house. "May I also have the honour of standing up with *you* for a set?" Both the rector's wife and her friend seemed delighted by his request, and he felt rather proud of himself for thinking of Mrs Collins.

Once the card table was placed and they were seated round it, Darcy had an opportunity to test both his patience and his abilities. He listened with half an ear to Mr Collins's prattle while trying to remember which cards had been played and which ones remained. Such undertakings were made more difficult while sitting across from his distracting partner, the partner he wanted for the rest of his life. He was grateful to Mrs Collins for agreeing to keep score. Darcy was an intelligent, masterly gentleman, but dealing with more than three or four tasks at a time was beyond even him.

Much later, as he stood with the others by the front door and donned his greatcoat, he remembered something else with which he had been tasked. "Miss Bennet, I believe you have something for me to deliver to my cousin's maid."

"Oh yes." She turned away. "I shall return directly with—"

"For shame, Cousin Elizabeth! Lady Catherine's nephew is not your personal courier!" Turning to his guest, Mr Collins begged pardon on behalf of his presumptuous relation.

There ensued then a bit of a commotion and fuss until Mrs Collins inserted herself into the fray.

"I shall fetch it for you, Eliza." Upon being told its location, she took her husband by the arm and led him away. "Do you not have that sermon to complete by tomorrow for Lady Catherine's approval?"

"Oh my *dear* Mrs Collins! You are so very..."

Their voices faded away, as did Darcy's surroundings. He had eyes and ears only for the couple's houseguest as she opened the door and glanced skywards.

"Finally, the clouds are clearing away. I can see the moon, a waxing crescent. There might even be a sunrise worth witnessing tomorrow."

While pulling on his gloves, Darcy took care to inform her there was a bench on a hill at the eastern edge of the park, a favourite spot of his, particularly in the mornings. Without thinking, he reached out and gently grasped her bare fingers, wishing he had not bothered with the gloves. Her eyes widened as she looked down at their joined hands, and his burgeoning smile fell flat. *Now that I am holding them, dare I kiss her fingers or simply give them a gentle squeeze?*

The ensuing awkwardness was dispelled by the return of Mrs Collins. Darcy released Elizabeth's hand to accept the valise stamped with her initials, then he bowed to both ladies.

"Good night. Thank you both for a most enjoyable evening." Plunking his hat upon his head, he stepped out into gathering darkness.

Being a gentleman, he resisted curiosity. Nothing could tempt him to violate Elizabeth's privacy by peeking inside the valise. Its contents would remain another mystery.

He ruminated then on their time together in Hertfordshire, back when he had foolishly thought a connexion to her and her family totally inappropriate. But that connexion, that attachment, that bond, was what he wanted more than anything in the world, and he could not help but reimagine a future together. Unreciprocated love and rejection might have broken his heart, but he would win hers, even if it took a lifetime. *Well, not a lifetime. I should like to raise a family with her before we are old and grey.*

Whatever boundaries she set would be respected, even though just being in her presence made his heart race. His stomach was often in his boots, and his grasp of the King's English sometimes failed him.

More awkward than when he was a stripling suffering from calf love over some young lady, being in love—truly in love—was a humbling experience.

Chapter Fourteen

Friday, April 17

Stars still shone when, bundled up warmly, Elizabeth left the parsonage.

After crossing the lane, she entered the frost-covered park and veered in an easterly direction. *I must be mad to leave my cosy bed at the merest crack of daybreak and walk in freezing temperatures towards the rising sun's weak warmth.* Despite that opinion, Elizabeth was as happy as a lark, though she did refrain from breaking into song.

Stepping lively and swinging her arms to generate heat, she gave herself free rein to think about Mr Darcy. He was not at all the vexatious, arrogant so-and-so she had been so prejudiced against since first acquaintance. His manner was so altered, so gentlemanly. He intently listened to what she had to say, behaved with propriety, smiled, and spoke to her more in the last se'nnight than he had during almost two months complete in Hertfordshire. With each and every encounter, her respect and regard had increased until his society was deemed entirely agreeable. And since there was nothing so tiring as ill temper, she was resolved to continue enjoying his company while unable to escape it. No, she no longer *wished* to escape it.

There he was just ahead also walking eastwards, coat-tails flapping in his wake. Elizabeth laughed at herself. *Just as I knew he would be.* Admiring his athletic frame, his confident, powerful stride and graceful carriage, she had to admit the gentleman was handsome, even from behind.

Previously, she had been plagued by the mischance that brought him to a place no one else but she ventured. That morning, though, she welcomed the opportunity to visit his favourite spot and to gradually improve the intimacy of their acquaintance far from prying eyes.

Hurried footfalls must have apprised him of her presence. Mr Darcy turned back, and she wondered if he had been listening for her. As he approached, Elizabeth's heart gave an unexpected lurch. Did it mean she held him in affection? She dismissed such a thought at once. The feeling, no doubt, was brought on by their forced proximity. It would not last once they returned to their customary lives.

Along with a greeting and a bow, he bestowed upon her such a broad smile that a dimple appeared upon his cheek. The good humour of his countenance made her breath catch, and the last vestiges of her pique fell through a crack in the ice of her heart and sank into murky depths, hopefully never to resurface.

He offered his arm, and mutual enquiries on common subjects passed before they walked awhile in silence, each unwilling to further disturb the dawn's quietude.

At their destination, which afforded a stunning view of the sun painting a rosy, golden glow across the cloudy horizon, Mr Darcy removed his greatcoat and spread it upon the bench's cedar planks. Then he stood, facing her and staring in evident admiration.

"Sir, you are missing the beauty behind you."

Without looking back, he replied, "It is unequal to the beauty before me—*your* light, *your* rosy glow."

Unaccustomed to compliments, Elizabeth bowed her head. Other appealing words, ones spoken eight days prior, resounded. *'...how ardently I admire and love you'*. Strong was her urge to reach out, to touch him, as he had done to her the previous night. In what? A gesture of affection? *Yes, perhaps.* She hoped her smile conveyed the happiness she felt.

He sat beside her then, close but not touching, and they chatted about their families and watched the colours change while the sun cleared the horizon.

With fondness and honesty, Elizabeth spoke of her parents. She sang her elder sister's praises and made excuses for her younger ones.

"Lady Catherine was quite put out that we had no governess and no accomplishments worth mentioning. Your aunt, of course, does not know that Lydia is a shining example to all young ladies."

"She is?" The disbelief in Mr Darcy's voice was almost comical.

"Oh yes. She is a shining example of how *not* to behave."

Tactfully dropping that subject, he asked, "And you? For what are you known? What is Miss Elizabeth Bennet's forte?" Although not another soul was in sight, he lowered his voice. "Other than capturing the master of Pemberley's heart, that is."

Until that moment, she had felt quite at ease, but when he said such things, what was she to say in return? "My grandest accomplishments are impertinent wit and an unerring ability to judge a person's character on first sight. 'Tis rather uncanny, really." In an admirable mimicry of Lady Catherine, she added, "I am quite proficient."

Pausing in indecision, Elizabeth fidgeted with a ripped stitch on her glove. "I wonder at my imprudence in asking this, sir, but if you ever were to return to Hertfordshire, would you—"

"Yes. Yes, I most certainly would, if you so wish it." He grinned.

Her application had begun in earnest, but Mr Darcy's unexpected playfulness tugged at her heart. "I was *going* to ask if you would consider becoming better acquainted with my family and relations. But now I shall not bother asking."

"Let us speak seriously, madam. If—no, *when*—I go there, I shall embrace your family, one and all. Figuratively, that is."

Elizabeth feared that if ever he *did* spend time with her family—notwithstanding what he had said to the contrary—his attachment would vanish faster than her youngest sister when there was mending to be done.

"I know your sister's name is Georgiana. Can you name mine?" *Will he meet my challenge?*

Without hesitation, he said, "Miss Bennet is Jane. Next would be Miss Mary, followed by Miss Catherine—though you called her Kitty, and Miss Lydia. But to be fair, you spoke of each by name just minutes ago." He leant forwards, his expression soft while looking deeply into her eyes. "I received a reply from Bingley, and your elder sister should expect a visit from my friend"—he consulted his watch—"in approximately seven hours."

Smiling and seeing him in a new light, Elizabeth barely stopped herself from embracing Mr Darcy. "Such rectitude, sir! You are the very best of men, and you have my heartfelt gratitude." Tears threatened, welling in her eyes as she imagined her beloved sister's happiness. A folded pocket-handkerchief appeared in front of her face. "Thank you. Oh, what is this?" A pink rose petal had fluttered from within the linen folds and landed upon her lap. "How lovely."

He seemed embarrassed. "It reminded me of your—" His eyes fell to her lips. "Of you."

Her blush matched the petal as she handed it to him. "In that case, you had best keep it. I would not want you to forget me."

"Never." His eyes sought hers. "Never could I, even if I tried."

The new light in which she viewed the gentleman shifted again in the sunrise, and it reflected the possibility of her own future felicity. Had Mr Darcy not previously alluded to the fact that he still wished to secure her affection, she would have sworn no man would offer marriage a second time to the same woman. No, she must not raise her hopes. *I fear I have become ill-fitted to endure the loss of his esteem.*

His adoring mien was becoming a little too intense, too intimate for Elizabeth's comfort. "It is fortunate your tidings about Mr Bingley bring me tremendous joy this morning, sir. There will be no need to shoot the messenger."

"I am glad to hear it." Shifting closer, he slid his arm along the back of the bench, his hand brushing her collar in the process.

Gooseflesh arose upon her nape. Her breathing was affected, and a thrill coursed through her entire body. That the staid Mr Darcy should affect her so! Keeping very still, she took a deep breath. *Whatever that fragrance is, he smells divine. Is it his shaving soap? What would he do if I just leant in and nuzzled that firm jaw?*

Thinking she might scream if he did not speak or *do* something, Elizabeth blurted the first thought that came to mind. "Anne seemed surprised when I made a remark about your being taciturn."

Withdrawing his arm, the gentleman smiled at her in a

self-satisfied manner. "You and Anne talked about *me*, did you?"

Looking down at the bothersome ripped stitch, Elizabeth hid a grin. "Yes. It must have been when we were rather desperate for a topic."

"Minx!"

Elizabeth tapped a forefinger against her chin. "I believe I was telling your cousin about the time I sat with a visitor at the parsonage, fearing we might sink into total silence. If memory serves, the gentleman took up a newspaper from the table, glanced over it, and made some sort of cold remark. Then Charlotte returned from her walk, and after sitting a few minutes longer without saying much of anything to anyone, the visitor went away."

"You are teasing me. And rightfully so." He rubbed his forehead a few times, and Elizabeth hoped she had not given him a headache. "I have made so many abominably stupid blunders since my father's demise, and I am so very sorry for any pain I have caused you."

Regretting that she had recounted the incident and suffering no little measure of shame over his woebegone expression, Elizabeth gave his arm three little pats. "Prepare yourself, sir. I am going to tell you something dreadfully shocking."

Expression grim, he nodded.

"You, Mr Darcy, are *human*. And humans make abominably stupid blunders all the time. *My* most recent one was when I just now mocked your past behaviour, and I beg your pardon for that. However, you must learn some of my philosophy." Drawing herself up, she gave him a stern look. "Repeat after me now, sir. Think only of the past as its remembrance gives you pleasure."

He complied, and his countenance softened into something akin to adoration.

Chapter Fifteen

Saturday, April 18

The oft-forgotten sitting room had been one of Sir Lewis's favourite sanctuaries at Rosings. The de Bourgh coat of arms was proudly displayed on the far wall, and the settee and its two matching armchairs were upholstered in blue fabric with a gold *fleur-de-lis* design. As Lady Catherine was fond of reminding everyone, her late husband came from a respectable, honourable, and ancient line.

On that Saturday, under cover of darkness in the wee hours of morn, actively engaged in their mischief, one pilferer turned to the other. "Do you not suffer even a modicum of guilt over these ill-gotten gains?"

A scoff was heard. "No," Dubois then whispered, "not at all. Belonging to our mistress, they are not ill-gotten. Why would I suffer guilt? We commit no sinister act, no crime causing bodily harm. We are not plotting to behead the King or blow up the House of Lords."

"Heaven forfend!" cried Mrs Jenkinson, a little too loudly.

"Hush, madam," Anne hissed at the elderly woman.

The five cushions with which Mrs Jenkinson was attempting to abscond were more than she could manage. Repeatedly, she dropped one, bent to retrieve it, complained about her rheumatism, and dropped another cushion in the process.

Unseen in the dim light, Anne rolled her eyes and practised patience. Mrs Jenkinson was still supposedly her companion. Soon, though, she would be, in Dubois's words, *de trop*.

Stepping up, Anne reminded Dubois that her uncle sat in the House of Lords. "Do not even *whisper* of blowing up one of our Houses of Parliament." She supposed her abigail, having left during France's Revolution of 1789, could not help but remember her country's ruthless atrocities.

Careful not to set anything aflame with her candle, Anne stooped to admire the settee and armchairs with all their gold-thread embroidery. *How I wish pieces of furniture were more portable!*

Softly saying, "Tassels! Tassels!" and bouncing from foot to foot, Anne's lady's maid pointed towards the curtains. With all that moving about, her candle flickered and extinguished.

Anne peered into the dark depths of the room. "Excellent, Dubois."

The abigail relit her candle from Anne's before fetching her scissors.

It is just as well the colonel departed when he did. Dubois had an admiring eye for not only Colonel Fitzwilliam's person but for his uniform's golden epaulettes.

Still, Anne was grateful to her maid. As a remedy for the ennui to which her mistress had succumbed earlier that year, Dubois had introduced *parfilage,* as it was known in her country. When the pastime reached England's shores, it was named drizzling. Stripping metallic threads from textiles caused tiny flecks of gold or silver to fall—like drops of drizzle—from their core of silk or linen.

Once popular with France's aristocracy, *parfilage* gave ladies the opportunity to exhibit graceful, elegant hand movements while picking precious threads from fabrics. In Anne's case, drizzling began as a lark but soon became an addiction.

"Well, ladies," she whispered as they gathered round. "Five cushions and a handful of tassels—a worthy yield for one night's work. I believe we now have all the thread I need to finish my creation." That clever idea had come about on the same day Anne had met Miss Elizabeth Bennet and noticed the formal drawing room's aureate cornice with its golden curves, spirals, and flourishes.

Guiding her accomplices out of the sitting room and up the staircase, Anne was sorry their lark was coming to an end. Although it all started as a harmless frolic with which to amuse themselves, she had learnt something useful in the process. She finally could proclaim herself an accomplished woman. Alas, no one other than Dubois and Mrs Jenkinson had witnessed her astounding feats of dexterity. *Soon, though, others will see how gracefully and skilfully I have used my hands.*

Only two days then remained until her twenty-first birthday, the celebratory ball, her surprise for a certain gentleman, and what would be shocking announcements for her mother.

Freedom and adventure were within sight. Giddiness increased apace.

So agitated by the promise of happiness, she scarcely could contain an urge to dash up the stairs and skip gaily along the halls.

Patience was not Anne's forte.

In a tiny sewing room while morning light shone upon the forgotten needlework on Anne's lap, she and Mrs Jenkinson listened enraptured as Dubois told them about the 'Field of Cloth of Gold'.

In June 1520, Henry VIII met France's François I in an attempt to ease the conflict between the rival kingdoms. With each monarch striving to outshine the other, the occasion became a magnificent spectacle with temporary pavilions, jousting, music, feasts, pageantry, and glittering tents and clothing of expensive fabrics woven with silk threads of silver and gold.

At least *Anne* listened to the splendour of it all while Mrs Jenkinson dozed by the fire. It was little wonder the elderly woman slumbered, considering their early morning ransacking of Sir Lewis's old sitting room.

The ballroom would not be quite so splendorous as a field of gold cloth, but Lady Catherine was sparing no expense to impress her guests and ensure their envy. *Let her. Most likely, it will be the last time my mother—or Rosings Park, for that matter—hosts such an event.*

Despite her grumblings to the contrary, Anne was fond of her mother. However, on the Fitzwilliam side of her family—with the exception of the colonel—there was an inherent arrogance she could not endure. And she supposed Darcy had inherited the same from his mother.

The de Bourghs, however, were neither titled nor did they feel in any way entitled. Instead of being imperious, they were fun-loving, adventuresome people. Anne missed them all. And, unfortunately, she was the last of that line of de Bourghs. It would end with her, as she was unwilling to have children of her own. It was not her intention to become maudlin that morning, however. Recollecting herself, she picked up the abandoned needle and resumed stitching while across the way Dubois added embroidery to another garment.

Lady Catherine had not seen her daughter's full-dress gown since witnessing its last fitting, a painful experience Anne still remembered well. Showing an abhorrent lack of respect, Dubois—miffed for some reason or other—had pricked her not once but several times with her nasty little pins. *I suppose I should be thankful it was not a guillotine.*

Anne assumed her mother still took for granted that the full-dress gown was the same pale, wholesome, unadulterated, bespoke garment they had commissioned in London months prior during a horrendous winter excursion. While the gown retained its modesty with no striking resemblance to Brinton's depiction, Dubois had altered it to better flatter Anne's small frame. *And the trim she worked onto it perfectly matches my eyes—at least according to my dear maid.* Daily, they prayed Lady Catherine would not demand another peek at the gown before the ball.

Having just then finished embellishing the robe, Dubois offered to lend her expertise to the item her employer was fashioning. Anne thanked her but declined. *The work must be mine and mine alone.* She was, quite literally, working her fingers to the bone to complete the garment.

Besides, Dubois had only a few days in which to add her magic to Miss Bennet's gown.

Time had grown short, and since most of those invited would not travel on the Lord's day, houseguests might start arriving at any moment, and her ladyship would expect Anne downstairs to receive them.

Making rapid stitches, she stabbed herself. A ruby-red droplet of blood beaded on the pad of her thumb. Staring at it, Anne grew lightheaded and clammy.

"Dubois, do fetch the salts. Everything is going quite… white. I fear I am going to…"

Chapter Sixteen

On the morning of the eighteenth, Darcy thanked God that Elizabeth had not departed for London as originally planned. *This past week would have been interminable without her.*

With cheerful eagerness, he greeted David, the footman stationed by the front door. Then he consulted his pocket watch and immediately regretted it. *Deuce take it! Not yet one o'clock.* He thought it rather vexatious that a gentleman was expected to adhere to proper morning call hours while visiting the lady he fully intends to marry and wake up with every morning.

Standing about like a statue and looking out the window, he thought he might write to his sister. Then he recalled that her most recent response had indicated her difficulty in keeping up with all the correspondence he had already sent.

So, it was either go for a brief ride, stay and play a solitary game of billiards, or give a few chapters of *St Irvyne* a second reading. He wondered why he had not thought to bring more books from his own extensive library. *Because I had not intended to remain here for such a duration, that is why.*

"Nephew!"

In the serenity of his own homes, Darcy was imperturbable. However, at Rosings, his aunt had an unsettling ability to startle him and disturb his peace.

"Where are you bound at this hour? You cannot be going for a ride attired like that, and it is too early for calls. No. You must remain within doors today. Anne and I shall need you on hand to help receive our houseguests. And of course, you will sit at the foot of the table as host."

But I do not want to be host. Strictly in his own mind, Darcy reverted for an instant to the spoilt little boy he had been before maturity, respect, and gallantry asserted itself. "But of course, Lady Catherine."

Later, having fetched *St Irvyne,* he ventured to the sitting room once preferred by Sir Lewis. Taking a seat by the window overlooking the kitchen gardens and berry bushes, he sat awhile, wondering why there were no cushions strewn about. *Must I report another incident to her ladyship?*

Just then, through the glass, his eye was caught by a familiar figure heading towards the servants' entrance. He bolted from the chair. *Gilchrist!*

Dashing down several staircases, he made his way through the maze of passages used by household servants.

Before Darcy could reach it, the door was flung open by a kitchen maid who said, "Oh my, Gilchrist." Twirling a curl round her finger, the young woman provocatively leant against the door jamb. "I thought you were dismissed."

Whatever the gardener said in return was missed as Darcy cleared his throat.

Turning at the sound, the blushing maid curtseyed and stammered. "Oh Mr Dar— Sir! I— Gilchrist here is asking for Miss de Bourgh."

Over my dead body! "I shall see to this. Thank you."

The gardener's eyes grew wide when Darcy appeared in the doorway. "What do you want, Gilchrist? And, no, you may *not* see Miss de Bourgh." It took an effort for him to remain civil.

In his Scottish burr, Gilchrist explained he was returning the gloves Miss de Bourgh had left at his bothy. He had found them, he said, while removing his belongings.

Accepting the proffered items, Darcy scoffed. "Oh really? Strange. Anne has not been out of the house for days. And the last time I was at your cottage, her herbarium was there, but her gloves were not. I gifted her these and would have noticed them there. So, are you Brinton's messenger now? I assume that is where my cousin left them. She was at Rara Avis five days ago and was not wearing her riding gloves when she left. No matter. I shall see that she gets them. Good day."

He closed the door and turned. The maid was still there, still red-cheeked, gaping at him.

"Return to your duties."

Why do members of the fairer sex blush in my presence? Darcy was neither stupid nor blind. He knew he was not ill-favoured.

His thoughts then flew to Elizabeth Bennet and her pretty blushes, and he prayed she would not suppose he was voluntarily absenting himself from her society. For his part, being deprived of her company was most wretchedly felt.

"Darcy!"

Does Lady Catherine lie in wait ready to pounce when I walk by?

Her ladyship had accosted him on his way from the billiards room to his cousin's apartments. Darcy had needed some form of physical release after his confrontation with Gilchrist.

"Why on earth are you carrying Anne's riding gloves about with you like that? Are you a mooncalf? Ah! I see." Her ladyship gave him a crisp nod. "I shall have Dubois cut a lock of my daughter's hair, though it would be more fitting if the request came from you."

That never will happen. "I was just about to have these gloves returned to Anne. She left them…somewhere."

"Where on earth is *some*where?" His aunt clutched her throat. "Were they found at Gilchrist's cottage?"

"They were not."

For but a moment, Lady Catherine's eyes closed in relief. "You must not disturb Anne at present. She is indisposed. The noble blood flowing through my daughter's veins means she is not as robust as those of the lower classes. Your poor cousin is so very fragile." She made a sad little sniff. "The dear girl needs a husband to look after her."

Why had I never before noticed the similarities between Mrs Bennet and Lady Catherine?

Faster than Wickham disappeared when there was work to be done, her tone shifted from compassion to authority. "Therefore, you will make your offer on Monday, and I shall announce the engagement at Anne's ball later that night." Lady Catherine gave a nod of supreme confidence. "Yes, that is how it must be done, and..."

Darcy let her prattle on. And prattle she did, without intermission, until her housekeeper came and requested clarification on which direction her ladyship wanted the folds in the table napkins to face.

His head throbbed, and Darcy realised he had not consumed nearly enough coffee to face the day.

After assisting the butler with the choosing of wines to serve during the celebratory supper, Darcy decided to station himself in the library. As requested by his aunt, he was to be readily available to cheerfully greet arriving houseguests. *An obligation I shall perform merrily and enthusiastically when pigs fly.*

He would, of course, be most welcoming and polite.

With a steaming cup of coffee at hand, he had just settled in a comfortable armchair and cracked open his book when a carriage was heard, followed by a rap of the knocker. He checked his watch. *By Jove! Where has the morning gone?* It was half past three o'clock.

The rest of Darcy's day was spent welcoming and conversing with various members of Kent's gentry and what seemed like a quarter of London's fashionable society. He prayed none of them had packed treasures to tempt the pilferer, whoever he or she might be. Images of all the trunks, portmanteaux, and valises being unloaded and sent to the guest wing made him cringe.

Because her ladyship wished to keep the distinction of her own rank preserved, excluded from the guest list were those of the aristocracy, the one exception having been the inclusion of the Earl and Countess of Matlock and their sons, the viscount and the colonel. Lady Catherine remained put out that none of those relations were available to attend.

Darcy regretted not only his male cousins' absence but also his own sister's. *Georgiana would not participate in the ball, but she could have met Elizabeth Bennet, her future sister.*

During that evening's dinner and afterwards in the drawing room, while Darcy's thoughts were half a mile distant, he fended off flirtations from Miss Harriet Roche, conducted under the watchful eye of her marriage-minded mother.

Chapter Seventeen

Sunday, April 19

On the quietest day of the week, there arose an uproar in the rector's home.

"But, my *dear* wife!" Flapping his wide-brimmed hat against his thigh, Mr Collins paced—if it could be called that—in mincing little steps. "Such shocking transgressions simply *must* be addressed in this morning's sermon."

Standing between her cousin and his wife, Elizabeth watched and listened as the previous evening's discord continued, her bonneted head turning one way then the other.

The lady of the house, also in pelisse and bonnet, calmly replied, "Having received Lady Catherine's approval of today's homily, you must not risk her displeasure by altering it now. Nor should you risk her indignation at having her misfortunes made public. She has not informed us of the situation and must wish it kept secret. Besides, it is merely hearsay."

"But I have heard the rumour from *three* unconnected sources. The thief or thieves responsible must be made to feel guilt and remorse and to make appropriate reparations." Sitting while the ladies stood, Mr Collins wiped his brow. "What a quandary! I dare not act in such a way as to incur the wrath of my patroness, however—"

Elizabeth consulted the mantel clock. "If I may interject, you certainly shall incur her ladyship's wrath if you dilly-dally much longer."

Her cousin's eyes grew wide as he confirmed the hour. Scrambling to his feet, he gave his wife a disapproving look. "My dear, you could have said so. Lady Catherine greatly objects to unpunctuality, and I shall never forgive myself if I have made her ladyship wait."

They reached the church with seconds to spare and to a nave packed with the faithful.

It seemed some, if not all, of Rosings Park's houseguests had arrived. With heels raised and weight upon the balls of her feet, Elizabeth quietly followed Mrs Collins, edging towards their assigned pew and feeling the disapproving eyes of not only Lady Catherine but the entire congregation upon her. Sliding across the highly polished wooden seat, she bowed her head and, beneath her brim, sought the one person she most wanted to see. *The one who did not call on me yesterday.* Notwithstanding that lapse, she felt somewhat appeased upon discovering his unwavering gaze fixed upon her, and she wondered what his deep blue eyes were trying to say.

Turning her attention to the assemblage, she noticed other rapt female eyes, young and old alike, resting not upon the perspiring rector but upon Mr Darcy's fine person.

His intense regard, however, had not strayed.

In the churchyard, while chatting with Mrs Jenkinson, Elizabeth watched Mr Darcy walk towards her. On his left arm was his cousin, on his right another young lady.

Despite being summoned by Lady Catherine, Anne simply gave her mother an acknowledging wave before leaving the other two behind, rushing forwards, and grasping Elizabeth's hands.

"Good day, my friend. I must not linger. Her ladyship grows increasingly restive and impatient. But Dubois has something for you, and she is just over there." Anne pointed out her maid's location. "Remember to fetch it before leaving. I am *so* looking forward to tomorrow evening!" She gave Elizabeth's fingers a squeeze. "Until then."

Mr Darcy then stepped forwards and bowed. "Miss Bennet, may I introduce to you Miss Harriet Roche of Brier Lodge in Westerham and currently a guest at Rosings. Miss Roche, it is my great pleasure to present to you Miss Elizabeth Bennet of Longbourn in Hertfordshire. She is a guest at Hunsford parsonage."

The two ladies curtseyed and voiced all the civilities and courtesies expected of genteel people, all the while assessing one another. At least Miss Roche was being judged, and she was found to possess a remarkable combination of symmetry, intelligence, and elegance. Elizabeth wanted to like her. *And I would like her…if she would just stop holding onto Mr Darcy's arm in the same manner my little cousin Michael holds onto his well-loved blanket.*

Mr Collins, lurking nearby, also seemed eager for Mr Darcy's attention, and Elizabeth feared he might introduce the rumour of Rosings Park's purported vandalism or theft.

When her cousin sidled up, bowing and scraping as was his obsequious wont, Mr Darcy curtly made the necessary introductions before saying, "Would you three please excuse Miss Bennet and me for a moment?" Without awaiting an answer, the gentleman bowed and removed Miss Roche's hand from his arm and replaced it with Elizabeth's.

"How I have missed you," he whispered, as they moved away. "Shall we walk the churchyard's perimeter, pretending we have some particular destination in mind, someone with whom we are desperate to speak? Just keep moving and smiling."

"Conveniently, I do have a destination, sir. Dubois has something for me."

"So be it." His gloved hand briefly and discreetly

covered hers. "I longed to call on you yesterday, but Lady Catherine kept me busy greeting houseguests. But enough of that. Are you well?" Beneath the lichgate, he stopped and stood before her. "Judging by that charming smile I so admire, I trust you are very well." His dimple made another rare appearance while he and Elizabeth gazed into one another's eyes.

"Nephew!"

She could not be sure, but Elizabeth thought Mr Darcy flinched. Beneath her fingers, she had felt the twitch of an arm muscle.

"Watch your step, young man!" The point of Lady Catherine's walking stick came perilously close to the gentleman's booted toes.

Letting go of his arm, Elizabeth surveyed the ground, expecting to discover a gaping chasm nearby or, at the very least, an angry adder, but the only evident danger appeared to be that pointy stick and the pointed look in Lady Catherine's eyes.

"Miss Bennet, it seems you are capable of leading astray not only my daughter but her intended as well." Her ladyship's chin was up, her neck exposed. "And as for you, Darcy, Anne and our houseguests await. Come now. I shall brook no opposition."

Squaring his shoulders, Mr Darcy spoke in a clipped tone. "I assure you, Miss Bennet has led no one astray. I shall be along directly, *after* I escort this decent, lovely lady to the parsonage. You may make my excuses to the others."

Lady Catherine huffed and walked away, nose in the air.

Elizabeth could not refrain from saying under her breath, "With her head held so high, Lady Catherine should be warned to watch her step."

Laughing aloud, Mr Darcy took up Elizabeth's hand, and she was certain he was going to kiss her gloved knuckles. Instead, he peeled back the cuff of her pelisse and brazenly placed his lips upon her wrist, and there they lingered until a feminine throat was cleared.

"It seems I am not the only one who has something for you, mademoiselle," said Dubois, grinning. She winked, handed the valise to Elizabeth, and turned away.

Face and neck flushed, Elizabeth fought an overwhelming desire to drop the bag and embrace her defender, the inimitable gentleman whose lips had lingered on her pulse, a kiss felt not only upon her wrist but in her heart.

"Clever lady," he said, watching Dubois walk away.

"Oh yes." Elizabeth nodded. "I quite like your cousin's maid."

"And me?" Mr Darcy stood close, very close, eyes only for her, the toes of his boots kissing hers. "Do you, perhaps, like *me*, even a little?"

Unbalanced, the scale of approbation had tipped heavily in his favour. "No, Mr Darcy." Elizabeth shook her head but leant in, smiling into his eyes. "I definitely do not like you a *little*."

* * *

After accompanying Elizabeth to the parsonage, Mr Darcy stood at the door, seemingly transfixed, eyes resting on her face with a remarkable expression of tender solicitude. "I do not like you a *little* either, Miss Bennet." He winked at her, then bowed over her hand. "Until tomorrow evening, madam."

Basking in the warmth of his affection, she watched until he vanished from view.

Eager then to discover whatever alterations Dubois had made to her gown, Elizabeth spent a few moments in polite conversation with Mr and Mrs Collins before inviting the latter to join her above stairs. Dashing up to her bedchamber while her friend followed more sedately, she opened the valise, withdrew the folded garment, and shook it free.

The lady of the house stood in the doorway, hands clasped beneath her chin. "Oh, how lovely! Is that the ivory gown you wore to the ball at Netherfield?"

"Yes. Yet it is not at all the same." Elizabeth held the garment against herself. "How does it look on me?"

Mrs Collins sat on the bed, reverently touching the blond gossamer netting. "As you know, I am not romantic and never was, but mark my words, tomorrow night you and that sumptuous garment will tug at Mr Darcy's heart-strings so strongly he will cleave to you and never let go."

Chapter Eighteen

Monday, April 20

He was enervated, and it was not quite a quarter past nine o'clock.

Darcy swore he never would forgive Fitzwilliam for being in the army, the viscount for being violently in love with a lady of the north, or the earl for being in Derbyshire. He was of the opinion that one of those gregarious Fitzwilliam men should have been there in his stead, playing host to the odd assortment of elegant, eccentric, and inebriated guests continually invading Rosings.

Still, there was no sign of Elizabeth although her contingent had the shortest distance to travel. Darcy's own coach had been dispatched to the parsonage to fetch them three tedious quarters of an hour ago, at about the same time as Lady Catherine's fit of pique over some drastic alterations that had been made to Anne's gown.

Farther down the hall, another clamour proved to the late arrival of the Hunsford party.

While footmen and maids accepted cloaks and hats, Lady Catherine and Anne greeted the party and accepted compliments on the latter's beautiful gown. Mr Collins, tripping over his words, upbraided his wife and cousin while simultaneously trying to exculpate himself and apologise to his patroness for their tardiness.

In no little agitation, Darcy strode towards them, and upon reaching Elizabeth, he bowed. "Good evening. Is everyone well? I thought your party might never arrive."

Tugging at an elbow-length glove, she gave him a playful smile. "Had I known you were so eager for my cousin's company, I would have suggested his second choice of cravat was superior to the first or third. Charlotte and I were already in our cloaks and waiting by the front door each time Mr Collins came down to ask his wife's opinion. Now it seems she and I are entirely to blame for our being tardy." She glanced at the others. "I hope Lady Catherine appreciates the effort he took on her account."

Smiling and looking at her intently, Darcy whispered near Elizabeth's ear, "You are the handsomest woman here." She was glorious in gold, as precious and as warm as the metal itself. How could any man fail to be affected by her loveliness? "An eternity stretches before me until I may claim your supper set. I doubt *you* will be without a partner all night, but I hope this evening may afford us an opportunity to engage in a private conversation." Invigorated by her presence, Darcy brought the lady's hand to his lips, thus marking his admiration.

"I shall count the hours, sir."

He had yet to release her hand. "Having agreed to stand up with Anne for the first set, I should go. Never before have I opened a ball, but hopefully I shall remember how the minuet is done. At her mother's insistence, my cousin is to call that old, stately dance." When the hired London musicians stopped tuning their instruments, he reluctantly said, "I must go."

Her gloved fingers slid from his, and she walked away.

Words raised in anger drifted again from the entrance door's direction. *Her ladyship.* Unable to place the calmer male voice, Darcy turned towards it.

Brinton! Why had he not considered the possibility of the master of Rara Avis being invited? Lady Catherine could not abide the man, so his cousin must have sent the invitation.

The newcomer, flourishing proof of his right to be there, wished felicity upon Anne, who soon hastened over to Darcy.

"Please, Cousin, do not let Mother turn him out." She cast a worried look over her shoulder as the commotion subsided. "Ah, it seems to be sorted now, and I believe Mr Brinton has just secured Elizabeth for the first set. Both being so terribly fond of dancing, they will be quite delighted with one another." She tugged on his arm. "Come, it is time for us to open this ball."

Ushering Anne to the ballroom, Darcy glowered at the gentleman accompanying Elizabeth. At another tug on his arm, he led his cousin to top position, all the while thinking Brinton would have been better off with a plain waistcoat rather than one with such gaudy, golden embroidery. *He is a popinjay with a ridiculous sense of fashion, at least compared to my austere style.*

Freezing in place as the minuet began, he recalled seeing something that very morning while re-examining the curtains in the back sitting room—*Dubois. By the berry bushes, handing something to Gilchrist. By Jove! Was it my indigo waistcoat?*

As Darcy and his cousin danced with controlled, ceremonious, graceful steps, he watched Brinton and Elizabeth doing the same. The deep blue fabric and gold embroidery of the gentleman's waistcoat perfectly matched that of Anne's open robe, and it could not be mere coincidence.

It was intolerable. Utterly galling!

After standing up with Mrs Collins, Darcy had danced the supper set with Elizabeth and had thoroughly enjoyed both the reel and her repartee, but following that delightful half an hour, as host, he was obliged to lead Lady Metcalfe into the dining room. Darcy sat at the lower end of the table with that lady at his right hand and Anne at his left, while farther up the table, Brinton had secured for himself a more delightful supper companion.

Throughout the evening, Lady Catherine had pestered Darcy about dancing a second set with her daughter, but he could not always be dancing, particularly with his cousin. It was, after all, his duty to ensure their guests' needs were being met, and each moment of that responsibility seemed to bring fresh agitation. Since there was a plethora of single gentlemen in attendance, other than his sets with Anne, Elizabeth, and Mrs Collins, he had not asked another to stand up.

From the corner of his eye, Darcy noticed his cousin's attention more often than not was taken up by the buzz of conversation taking place amongst Brinton and those nearest him. *I, not he, should be sitting next to Elizabeth, engaging her in conversation, pouring her wine, serving her delicacies, earning her smiles.*

Brinton, turning towards Elizabeth, placed his hand on the back of her chair and made a remark that instigated sweet laughter. Darcy wondered of what they spoke, knowing he never could compete with the man's sarcastic wit. *Brinton is too exuberant, too theatrical, and too vibrant, while I am restrained.*

After absently serving portions of flummery to Lady Metcalfe and Anne, Darcy trained his eyes again on the gentleman serving Elizabeth.

I should like to knock the spoon from the popinjay's hand and bounce it off his head, flummery and all. Stifling a sigh, he smiled at whatever Lady Metcalfe had just said to him.

Half an hour later, as a hush descended over the room in anticipation of Darcy's speech, he discerned a boisterous remark extolling Elizabeth's appeal.

"Miss Bennet," cried Brinton, "has thrown me into unceasing delight tonight with her uncommon union of grace, brilliancy, and wit."

Darcy rolled his shoulders and watched Elizabeth lift a glass to her lips. He supposed the sip of wine was meant to either conceal the fine blush overspreading her cheeks or to wash away the bad taste such extravagant praise had left in her mouth. She seemed so awkwardly circumstanced that Darcy's heart cried out to hold her close. *Beyond the pale! A gentleman flatters delicately, never in a forward or intrusive manner. Clearly, Brinton's attentions are making her increasingly uncomfortable.*

Desperate to intercede, Darcy was compelled to remain in his place and propose a toast congratulating Anne on having reached the age of majority. *Quite an accomplishment, apparently.*

The instant that duty was performed and the grand dining room and adjoining parlour began to empty, Darcy saw Elizabeth stand abruptly, say something to the others, curtsey, then walk out of the room. He signalled David, the footman, and quietly ordered him to keep a discreet eye on Miss Bennet and ensure her well-being.

Consoling himself with the fact that *he*, not Brinton, would have the honour of standing up with her for the final set, Darcy lost no time in striding over and taking the seat Elizabeth had occupied.

"Brinton, a word." Accepting a decanter of port from a footman, he poured two glasses and handed one to the younger gentleman. "Your voice carries, and I could not help but overhear your comments to Mrs Godsell about Miss Bennet. To speak in such extravagant praise is inappropriate at the best of times but particularly ill-suited to a supper table. Did you not take into account the discomfort of those two ladies or the others within your proximity?"

Brinton's eyes narrowed. "Never could I be like you, so rigidly opposed to anything not dictated by decorum and formality. Why is it wrong for an artist, or any man, to admire a beautiful woman? Do you not think Miss Bennet a darling in every feature and every gesture?"

To himself, Darcy admitted he, that very night, had wondered how any man could fail to be affected by her loveliness.

Slouching a bit, Brinton seemed absorbed in his own thoughts of her. Then, sitting up, chin jutted, he declared, "Miss Bennet will be my Muse, and I shall capture her radiance in oils, in song, and in verse." He slid his untouched glass towards Darcy. "I no longer partake of either alcohol or opium, remember? I am entirely happy without them. Life is to be lived, not tranquillised." Gaining his feet, he added, "By the bye, I am thrilled to have Gilchrist back in my employ. I was sorry to lose him after he and I had a little tiff around this time last year. Now, if you will excuse me, I am in pursuit of inspiration."

Back in the ballroom, Darcy prowled about in search of

Elizabeth. He checked his pocket watch. Two o'clock. Two dozen couples were in place, ready to recommence the dancing, which he feared would continue for five more hours, at which time breakfast would be served.

What a devilishly long night! Though small talk was the bane of his existence, he exerted himself to mingle awhile, reminding people of the availability of tea, wine, negus, orgeat, and cake. Weaving in and out amongst a milling crowd of more than one hundred guests, he caught whiffs of perfume and perspiration as well as snatches of gossip he would rather not have heard.

Amidst the general hubbub, a lively Scotch reel began, and the floor shook from all the fancy footwork. Craning his neck, Darcy looked over the horde. His cousin was standing up with Mr Tottle.

But where is Elizabeth? She was not dancing. He was taller than most, still he could spot neither her brunette curls nor pale gold gown. There also was no sign of either Brinton or the assigned footman.

Extending his search, he moved room to room and asked those acquainted with her if they knew Miss Bennet's whereabouts. None of the ladies had seen her in any of the rooms in which they occasionally sought comfort, and Darcy's manners were at once deprived of their usual composure. Returning in haste to the ballroom, he reached his cousin just as Mr Tottle was escorting her to a chair.

"Anne, have you seen Miss Bennet recently?"

When she replied she had not, Miss Roche, standing

nearby, said, "I have. She ran up the main staircase not five minutes ago." She tittered behind her fan. "With Mr Brinton hard on her heels."

Unsavoury images pressed upon Darcy's thoughts and sent his heart racing.

Chapter Nineteen

Moving with haste through the manor's maze of dim galleries and long, unlit passages, Elizabeth expected to encounter a maid or a footman, but she supposed they were bustling about below.

She turned another corner. Nothing looked familiar. It was just as she had predicted days ago, and she despaired of ever finding her way. Why on earth had she run instead of seeking Mr Darcy or Mr Collins? Was she a stranger to common sense? At least she seemed to have escaped Mr Brinton.

Having worked herself into a state of distress at that gentleman's persistent pursuit, she had made the excuse of needing to fetch something from her cloak in the ladies' retiring room. *Which is not above stairs. So why did I stupidly follow Miss Roche's misdirection? What am I doing up here? And where is the elusive staircase?*

At supper, Mr Brinton had flattered her beyond reason. Then, in the ballroom, he had importuned her about capturing her likeness in oils. Going on and on about what a vision she was in that gossamer gold netting, he had been insistent on her wearing it while sitting for the portrait. The slightly indecent one of Anne had come to mind, and Elizabeth presumed the artist meant for her to wear the netting and nothing more.

Descrying a sliver of light escaping beneath a door and surmising someone must be within, Elizabeth ran towards the glow, her spirits rising apace. When lightly tapped, the ajar door creaked open, and she stumbled inside, eyes adjusting to the light of a lantern and candles.

"Dubois! Oh, I am so *very* glad to see you. I beg your pardon for invading your bedchamber."

The room was tiny. Spools of metallic threads glittered in the candlelight, and through a window, the waxing gibbous moon illuminated stacks of cushions in a corner.

"This is a sewing room, Miss Bennet." The lady's maid frantically stuffed bobbins and shuttles into work baskets and bags. Looking then towards the doorway, she wrung her hands. "Are you alone?"

"Yes," replied Elizabeth.

"No," said a deep, male voice.

After thanking someone named David, Mr Darcy stepped inside the room.

Soft, hurried footfalls from the hall padded closer, and the three inside turned in their direction. Rounding the doorway, Anne was stopped short by her cousin's chest.

"Darcy!" She rubbed her nose and sounded indignant. "What are you doing here?" Peering round him, she gasped. "And Elizabeth!" Shoulders slumped, she heaved a sigh. "Well, Dubois, I believe our bit of sport has come to an end."

Mr Darcy shook his head at her. "I suspected the perpetrator was a young lady with no notion of a waist-coat's worth, but I never suspected *you*...until earlier tonight." He pulled something from his fob pocket. "I believe this is yours, Anne." A gold guinea gleamed in his hand.

"I do not understand." Elizabeth frowned. "Oh! Is this about the thievery?"

Anne stamped her foot in its dainty dancing slipper. "It is *not* thievery! Any gold threads removed from this manor's textiles belong to *me*, and I care not a fig if a few fripperies and cushions do not glitter as brilliantly as before." Under her breath, she added, "Besides, all of this soon will seem utterly inconsequential."

Elizabeth held a section of her gown's netting up to a candle. Gossamer, pale blond silk shimmered. Darker gold embroidery glinted in reflected light. "Are these—"

"Yes, madam." In a sardonic tone, Darcy said, "I suspect the golden threads forming those pretty little flowers were extracted from cushions in what once was Sir Lewis de Bourgh's favourite room."

Even in dim light, Elizabeth's embarrassment was evident. "Is that true, Anne? Am I attending an elegant private ball wearing pieces of your late father's *cushions*?" Palms covered her face.

"They look beautiful on you," Mr Darcy said, Anne echoing the sentiment.

Elizabeth's shoulders shook, and the others offered comforting words until Anne cried, "Elizabeth Bennet, are you *laughing*?"

"Yes! Yes, I am. And as Mr Darcy knows, I dearly love a laugh."

Darcy whispered something in Anne's ear. She nodded and took a fond look about the room.

"Come along, Dubois. Our work here is done." To her cousin and Elizabeth, she said, "Do not linger, you two. I have something of paramount importance to relate to my mother, and I should like both of you there with us."

Once mistress and maid had gone, Mr Darcy turned to Elizabeth. "I have an apology to make. You were distressed earlier by something Brinton said or did, and I did not rush to your aid. Please forgive me." He took up her gloved hand in his. "I swear with my life and until the end of my days, if you would allow it, I will care for you and safeguard you whenever you need protection."

Love swelled until Elizabeth feared her heart might burst. "I understand you had other duties, sir, and I am beginning to suspect I was in no peril at all. In fact, I would be surprised if there is not some sort of scheme afoot. Did you happen to notice that your cousin's robe perfectly—"

"Matches Brinton's waistcoat? Yes, I did. But enough

about them." Mr Darcy had yet to release her hand. "Let us not waste this golden opportunity, Miss Bennet. I wish to now have that private conversation alluded to earlier." His voice had become husky, and he cleared his throat. "Every night for the past eleven days, I prayed to God that you might remain a part of my life and that I may be welcomed into yours—to be your friend, to laugh with you, and to wipe every tear that falls."

With a hoarse voice quavering with emotion, he begged her pardon. "I have spoken so much in the past few days that I fear the words I wish to say to *you* might remain forever lodged in the back of my throat."

"If you are like other gentlemen and carry a flask in that coat, I shall not object if you take a sip."

He thanked her and turning away, did just that. Facing her again, he reclaimed her hand and admitted he had first admired her at Lucas Lodge. "Each succeeding encounter built upon that initial admiration until it became immoveable affection. Even after you refused me, I knew you were the only woman in the world whom I could ever be prevailed on to marry."

Elizabeth blushed to hear her own words repeated back, but the fervent, burning look in his eyes told her she was loved.

"You are more precious than all the gold in the world, and I— I love you." More emphatically, he repeated, "I *love* you."

Those three words produced in her the tremors of a most palpitating heart. Tears welled in her eyes, and unable to help herself, she sniffed as a salty drop slid down her cheek.

"Here, now," Mr Darcy whispered, wiping it away. "This is not the time for tears...unless they be mine should you say no."

"To what, sir?" She sniffed again. "You have yet to ask a question."

"Then let me be explicit. Miss Elizabeth Bennet, may I be your husband? Will you be my wife, my helpmate, my partner? Will you share with me life's joys and sorrows? Will you be my lover and the mother of my children? Will you grow old with me? Will you stand with me before an altar and say I will?" He waited. "*Now* would be an excellent time to say yes."

"Yes!" She was laughing; she was crying. "Yes, *I will* marry you, Mr Darcy."

"My heart is yours," he whispered, though no one else was near.

"I shall carry it with me for evermore."

With a stuttering intake of breath, she felt his hand on her nape, drawing her closer. Then his mouth was on hers, tender and tasting of brandy and of heavenly delight. When both his hands cupped her face, the kiss contained all the pent-up passion of the past five months.

Her sentiments towards him were all that was respectful, tender, and exquisite. *I love him to the utmost, to the very top of the cup, quite brim-full!*

From the ballroom far below, music grew louder, the cadence faster.

Mr Darcy stepped back and extended his hand. "Do you not feel a great inclination to dance a reel?"

Throwing back her head, Elizabeth laughed.

In that sewing room with faces beaming, Elizabeth and Mr Darcy danced. Golden threads in the floral hem of the lady's gown sparkled by candlelight.

The smile on his face had not subsided. "I have not felt so young, so alive, so carefree since boyhood." He stopped dancing. "Dearest Elizabeth, how I love you!"

"And I love you, dear sir, not merely a *little*." When he remained silent, she asked if he was not diverted.

"Oh yes. I am diverted. Diverted by that smile. Diverted by those lips as soft as rose petals." He dipped his head towards Elizabeth's mouth.

"Ahem." The voice belonged to a fair-haired young footman whose face grew increasingly red. "I beg your pardon, but Miss de Bourgh requests your presence in the back parlour."

Mr Darcy whispered in Elizabeth's ear, "Let Anne wait." Again he determinedly dipped his head to her lips.

Epilogue

April 20, 1822

In the mistress's rarely used bedchamber at Pemberley, while Elizabeth and Benjamin slept, Darcy attempted to attend to his book.

It was a futile effort. Try as he might, he could not concentrate on Virgil's *Georgics*. What were ancient agricultural verses to one's newborn son?

Setting aside the poem, he carefully moved towards the cradle to peer yet again at the precious, dark-haired bundle nestled therein. *Could life possibly supply any greater felicity than this?* Crouching, he set the rockers in gentle motion.

He was no novice to fatherhood. The infant was their fourth child and second son. Following each birth, Darcy's heart had filled to overflowing with love and gratitude for his extraordinary wife—mother of Anna, William, Isabelle, and little Benjamin.

At a rustle of bedclothes and a whimper from across the room, he rushed to Elizabeth's side.

"Fitzwilliam, have the Brintons arrived?" Drowsy, she shifted on the mattress and grimaced. "My timing—or rather, our perfect but impatient son's early arrival—could not have occurred during a more inconvenient week."

Darcy placed a lingering kiss upon his wife's forehead, then took his seat at her bedside. "Rest easy, my love. The travellers have yet to arrive. However, while their husbands play poorly at billiards, Georgiana and Jane have everything and everyone under good regulation—with the assistance of one governess, two nursery maids, and our new housekeeper-in-training, all under the watchful eye of dear old Mrs Reynolds. At present, my dear Mrs Darcy, *your* only duties are to recover and, of course, to nourish Ben." Drawing her hand to his lips, he pressed a kiss upon Elizabeth's fingers.

Elizabeth held fast to Darcy's hand. "I am certain time means little at all to the Brintons. They, Dubois, and Gilchrist are dictated to by clocks only when they must catch a ship or some such conveyance. As Anne has written, our time on earth is far too short. Life is to be lived in the present. Tomorrow holds no guarantees."

As well I know. Each of his intrepid wife's labours to bring a child into the world had filled Darcy with terror.

"What is the time?" Elizabeth squinted at the clock

upon the mantel. "Anne promised they would arrive today."

"'Tis not yet eleven." Darcy stood and fussed with her coverlet. "Sleep now, my darling. Anne will no doubt dash up here to see you before a maid can even remove her pelisse. By the bye, our little Anna hopes, in her own words, 'Mr and Mrs Brinton will come bearing gifts from afar'."

Elizabeth sighed. "I suppose that is my fault for telling Anna about Rara Avis and its many treasures. I also read to her the Brintons' descriptions of lands of incredible sights, sounds, and smells." Rubbing sleepy eyes, she mumbled, "Briny sea breezes in Tuscany…cinnamon and saffron in Constantinople…the clean, crisp, piney air of the Swiss Alps…"

Darcy bent and placed another kiss on Elizabeth's brow as she drifted towards slumber. "I shall take you to all those places one day, my dearest love."

Hours later, propped up against downy pillows while suckling Benjamin, Elizabeth took a sip of barley water and listened to Anne Brinton—née de Bourgh—who sat upon the bedside chair.

"Benjamin is beautiful, truly. You know I never wanted children of my own, but Laurence and I are honoured that you and Darcy asked us, along with Mr Bingley, to be Ben's godparents. I am certain we shall spoil him terribly."

"Indeed. I have heard about the rocking horse, the pewter soldiers, and a toy theatre complete with scenery. Anna was thrilled with the doll you brought her and all the little gowns for it. I particularly liked hearing about the gold one with floral embroidery in metallic threads." Elizabeth gave her a pointed look.

"Hah! I should like to claim credit for that, but Dubois made it with, I believe, some old scrap of fabric from the year twelve." Anne heaved a sigh. "Can you credit the passage of exactly a decade since my celebratory ball?"

"Not at all." Elizabeth stifled a yawn. "Yet, so much has happened in both our lives during those intervening years." Benjamin's nurse lifted the sleeping babe from his mother's loving arms. "Remind me again of what transpired that night at Rosings. Especially," Elizabeth added with a grin, "while your cousin and I were more agreeably engaged in the sewing room."

"Humph! You mean while I was worried sick about what might have been keeping the two of you." Anne winked, then poured herself a glass of Elizabeth's citrus-flavoured barley water.

"A maid should be here directly with refreshments."

"No, no. This is fine. Now, as I remember it, while most of my guests were in high revel, I asked Mrs Jenkinson to have my mother meet me in Father's old sitting room. When her ladyship arrived and had taken a seat, I told her I was to be wed. Ecstatic, she assumed I meant to Darcy. When I said, 'No, not my cousin,' Mother flew into a rage."

Anne set aside her glass, and in a credible imitation of Lady Catherine's voice, cried, "'Heaven and earth, child! *You* cannot wed a man of inferior birth and no importance in the world. This match, to which Gilchrist has the audacity to aspire, can never take place. Such an alliance would be a disgrace. Honour, decorum, and prudence forbid it. I am ashamed of you for even thinking it.' My scheme had gone according to plan, but I felt dreadful all the same. 'No, Mother,' I said to her, 'not Gilchrist.'

"My mother was at once both relieved and suspicious, and she asked, '*Who,* then?' Laurence must have been waiting outside the door because he walked in then and bowed to her ladyship. His tailcoat was open, and his thumbs were hooked in the pockets of the indigo waistcoat—the one I had taken from Darcy's dressing room and lovingly embroidered with golden threads. It had been my engagement gift for him."

Elizabeth nodded. "Ah yes, those infamous golden threads."

The maid entered with a tea tray, and Anne poured two cups and passed one to Elizabeth. "Laurence had liked the waistcoat and praised my embroidery skills. Later, though, when he discovered from whence those golden threads had come, he helped me understand why *parfilage* was wrong. People far less fortunate than I had toiled long hours to create the beautiful tapestries, curtains, cushions, and such that I so thoughtlessly ruined. Similarly, on our trips abroad, my husband disparages travellers who purloin another country's antiquities."

Elizabeth reached over and squeezed Anne's hand. "As you once told me, Mr Brinton is a rare bird."

"Oh, that he is! Laurence thinks highly of you, Elizabeth, but back then his interest in you was a ruse, as was mine in Gilchrist. Of course, Mother was put out that I was to wed Brinton, not Darcy. Her ladyship did not care for the master of Rara Avis. He was too free-spirited for her liking. She, however, could not object as violently to a wealthy gentleman as she had to a gardener. The scheme Laurence, Gilchrist, and I had concocted—the impression of a liaison with my master gardener—had succeeded. I would have married Laurence nevertheless, with or without Mother's consent. I was twenty-one years of age then, had reached my majority, and no longer required her permission. Still, I had hoped for her blessing. Then, when I revealed our other plans, she was at no pains to conceal her vexation or repress the peevishness of her temper. '*Sell* Rosings Park? No. I shall not have it!'

"Referring to her as such for the first time in my life, I said, 'Mama, you are correct. *You* will not have it. Rosings is mine, and Mr Brinton and I have decided to sell. You and Mrs Jenkinson may live in the dower house or in London. Provisions have been made for such accommodations.' Laurence then placed his hand upon my shoulder and said, 'Lady Catherine, what would your daughter and I do with this pile? We have Rara Avis. Besides, it is our plan to travel abroad for years.'

"My mother then cried, 'Travel abroad? For years? Heaven and earth! What about children?' I remember taking a deep breath, then my words rushed forth. 'There will be no children to inherit either Rara Avis or Rosings.' Aghast, her ladyship shrieked, 'No children? Stars and garters, Anne! It is a woman's duty to give her husband children.' Laurence supported me by saying, 'Your daughter and I are in complete agreement. There will be no children.'

"Taking her hands in mine while she sat there in gloomy dejection, I said, 'Mama, I apologise for ruining your ball and for disappointing your hopes. Nevertheless, I am resolute.'

"That is when you and Darcy *finally* made an appearance. But apart from Laurence and me standing up together for a third set, followed by the announcement of our engagement, all had been said and done by that point.

"At least Mother lived to see me married." Anne sniffled. "How I wish I had been able to say my last farewell to both her and Mrs Jenkinson, but we were in Greece by then. I still mourn them."

A tap sounded at the door, and the nurse, holding Benjamin, opened it to admit her employer. The proud father relieved the woman of her burden and told her to take a short respite.

"I have come with a summons from your husband, Anne. You are to leave poor Elizabeth alone and repair to your own chambers to dress for dinner. Had you not bolted up here before being shown to your quarters, you might now know where to find your dressing room and Brinton. Fortunately for you, the footman stationed beyond this door can be of service in that endeavour." Darcy smiled at his cousin while making a shooing gesture.

Alone with her husband and their youngest child, Elizabeth reached out, inviting them to join her on the bed. "How I wish I could dress for dinner and join everyone."

Well, not everyone. Mama and Papa remain at Longbourn with the Collinses. No one is happy with that arrangement, but Papa is failing, and his heir needs preparation for taking his place. Mary and her husband are settled in Meryton, and Captain and Lydia Carter are who knows where. Elizabeth's youngest sister foolishly had set her cap for Mr Wickham, who was subsequently taken by a press gang and shipped to Lower Canada. Lydia then set her sights higher. Colonel Fitzwilliam, however, remained a bachelor, and she settled for a captain in the regulars.

Holding Benjamin, Darcy carefully settled beside Elizabeth and kissed her cheek. "Everyone understands, love." He bestowed a reverent kiss atop the babe's head before shifting him to his shoulder. "Oh, the Marshalls have arrived. Kitty should be in to visit you and her newest nephew any minute now." He gave Elizabeth a look of disgust as Benjamin spit milk onto his superfine coat.

She laughed. "You should be well accustomed to that by now, Fitzwilliam, although it has been two and a half years since Isabelle last did that to you."

Initially, Elizabeth could not understand Anne's decision to remain childless, that is until Darcy explained that the Brintons had a peculiar sort of marriage of convenience. Anne's husband and Gilchrist were more than employer and master gardener. They were *friends*. While an under-gardener tended plant life at Rara Avis, Gilchrist accompanied the Brintons on their journeys and collected botanical specimens for their estate. While the men were otherwise occupied, Anne and Dubois saw the sights, shopped, and sampled local cuisine. Together, the four of them made memories, going wherever the breeze took them, quenching their thirst for new places and new experiences. Opportunities, they said, were everywhere.

Content to remain at Pemberley until her children were grown, Elizabeth knew she and Darcy would travel eventually, perhaps with their sons and daughters, perhaps just the two of them.

In the meantime, she snuggled against her husband's side and, catching a whiff of his shaving soap, nuzzled his firm jaw.

"Mr Darcy," she whispered, "you must allow me to tell you how ardently I admire you, how greatly I respect you, and how very passionately I love you. Now and for evermore."

"Even when we are old and grey, Mrs Darcy, I never will grow tired of hearing—"

Benjamin's lusty wail spoilt the moment, but his very presence was testament to his parents' grand and everlasting love.

The End

Acknowledgments

The brilliant ladies at Quills & Quartos are the absolute best. It’s true! So I‘m taking advantage of this golden opportunity (see what I did there?) to thank Amy D’Orazio and Jan Ashton for not only their extraordinary editing expertise but for the caring and professional manner in which they conduct their publishing business.

About the Author

J Marie Croft (Joanne) is a life-long resident of Nova Scotia, Canada, but spends a lot of time in Regency England with Jane Austen's beloved characters. She has written eleven Austenesque stories. Joanne shares with her husband a love of their adult twin daughters, the great outdoors, geocaching, and a spoiled calico cat.

facebook.com/jmarie.croft

bookbub.com/authors/j-marie-croft

amazon.com/stores/J.-Marie-Croft/author/B004HZD22W

Also by J Marie Croft

Enduring Connexions

I love you with so much of my heart that none is left to protest— William Shakespeare

WHEN FITZWILLIAM DARCY IS BETRAYED by love at the age of twenty-three, he vows that never again will he allow a woman to own his heart. Never again will he be made a fool. Never again will he trust. His heart and pride will be spared from another crippling blow, no matter what.

FOUR YEARS LATER, his resolve is put to the test. Elizabeth Bennet is vivacious and beautiful, but she has family connexions which make her unsuitable for him. Her immediate family is vulgar, and her relations are involved in trade. Worst of all, she has an elder sister, Jane, who is nearly a twin of the woman who broke his heart and shattered his trust. Yet, despite his reservations, Darcy's growing affection for Elizabeth is impossible to deny or resist.

ALAS, JUST AS DARCY BEGINS TO ALLOW the walls around his heart to crumble, a dark secret from someone else's past comes to light and threatens the stability of the Bennet family's very foundations. A connexion Darcy could never have imagined will have a potentially devastating impact on the Bennets and on his and Elizabeth's burgeoning love. If Darcy wants Elizabeth in his life, he and the Bennets must learn to forgive and accept that which cannot be changed.

Made in the USA
Coppell, TX
17 February 2024

29093578R00105